TOURNAMENT OF LOSERS

Tournament of Losers
By Megan Derr

Published by Megan Derr

Edited by Samantha M. Derr
Cover designed by James, GoOnWrite.com

For Piper, of course <3

TOURNAMENT OF LOSERS

MEGAN DERR

FIFTEEN SLICK

Over the course of thirty-three years, Rath had been woken up in a number of unpleasant ways.

Being dragged out of bed by angry people out for his blood was his least favorite. That included the time someone had thrown boiling water on him and left him with burns that had taken ages to heal.

He grunted as his head was slammed against the floor again, kicking out wildly, somewhat mollified by the pained cry of the goon he managed to hit. Getting to his feet, Rath started swinging, and he was big enough and swung hard enough that the overeager assailants finally backed off.

Then someone bigger got a good knock in, and Rath dropped to his knees, disoriented, pissed off, and entirely too hungover to do much about it.

"Good morning, Rat."

Well, that narrowed down *who* was after him. *Why* was still unclear, though he could make a damned good guess. Rath dragged his eyes up, keeping his roiling stomach under control only from long years of practice, and glared through bleary eyes at the large-ish man looming over him like a gilded manor.

A gilded manor soaked in enough perfume to drown a whorehouse, but nobody said that to the Friar of East End if they wanted to keep their teeth. "Good morning, Friar."

Friar smiled bitingly. "Not such a good morning for you and yours."

"If you've bothered my mother about this—"

"I do not bother ladies unless absolutely necessary," Friar cut in, scoffing as though he'd never committed an act of violence in his life, let alone against a woman.

Rath rolled his eyes. "I'll believe that never. How much does my worthless father owe you this time?"

"Fifteen marks, in three days."

That was enough to knock the last dregs of sleep and alcohol right out of Rath's system. "Why the buggering *fuck* does my shit father owe you fifteen slick?" Even if Rath earned a steady income every working day of the year, which he definitely didn't, he wouldn't make more than just over two slick. What had his father *done?* Rath was going to kill him for real this time.

"Oh, I don't want to ruin the fun he'll have explaining." Friar patted his cheek. "You should have agreed to work for me back when you were worth something, Rat. You know where to find me when you have the money. You have today, plus three, because I'm feeling just the slightest bit sorry for you. Have it to me by final bells." He signaled sharply to the other figures in the room.

The massive figure who'd knocked Rath to his knees gave him a parting shove to the floor. He glared at her. "Always a pleasure, Jen."

Jen gave him a smile full of malice and silver teeth, then was gone with the slamming of the door.

As morning wake-ups from Friar went, that could have gone worse.

"What in the world was that all about?"

Oh, right. Between the rude wake-up and being told his days were numbered *again* if he didn't come up with an alarming sum of money *again*…

"Nothing," Rath replied and gingerly picked himself up off the floor, holding fast to the rickety bedpost, swaying slightly, but managing not to fall.

He looked at the handsome man still in bed, all dark skin, long, dark, braided hair, and eyes green enough to make an emerald mad with jealousy.

"Who was that?" the man asked.

Rath wished he could remember the man's name, but right then, he was lucky to remember his own. Oh, what he wouldn't give for a mug of ale or six. But he was about to be a little too busy for that. "If you don't know, then count your blessings and keep stupid questions to yourself. I'm sorry to go, beautiful, but there's much to be done and very little time to do it."

The man waved a hand dismissively. "I hope you're able to come up with the money." He flopped back down on the bed, which creaked under his weight and careless treatment. "Be a shame for the world to lose a man of your talents."

"Hopefully, the Fates agree with you. *Ta, darling,*" Rath replied, mimicking the man's High City accent. He found his clothes and pulled on his stockings, breeches, and boots. Snatching up his shirt and jacket as he clambered to his feet, Rath checked that the coins hidden in the jacket were still there. "I hope you find your way back to High City without trouble. Hide your purse."

The man laughed and gave a lazy wave, clearly more interested in going back to sleep.

Fun while it lasted. Pity it couldn't last most of the morning. Ah, well. Best to put away distracting thoughts. Rath pulled his shirt on as he stepped into the hall, then shrugged into his jacket. It was going to need a patch on the left elbow soon; he could feel the fabric about to give out.

Out in the street, the smell of cheap food from various carts lining the street and in front of the bridges turned his stomach. He started out going north, bound for the common bridge, one of three that spanned the channel that cut the city roughly in two. The top third, north of the bridges, was reserved for the hoity-toity, called High City. The other two-thirds, south of the bridges, was for everyone else, called Low City. The three bridges were formally called after the women who had been in charge of their building: Sherenda, Herth, and Martiana. But they were generally called the guard bridge, the common bridge, and the private bridge, which was also called the holy bridge, because the lords and ladies certainly acted like they were holier than everyone, up to and including the gods.

By the time Rath had hauled through the city to the common bridge, his stomach had calmed down, but his headache had tripled in agony. Thankfully, the food vendors by the bridge always had food they were willing to sell cheap to the locals; it cost him only a farthing for a bit of cheese and bread with honey. Foreigners would be conned out of at least a whole penny, and some of the really good vendors could get as much as two.

"Hale, Rath!"

He looked up at the cheerful voice and smiled at the man who came running toward him, shirt unlaced, breasts unbound, hair tumbling about his shoulders. "Did you get thrown out of some lady's room, to be running around half-dressed?" Rath asked and offered half of the honey-slathered bread he'd bought.

"Maybe," the man muttered and wolfed down the food. "Worth it, though. You should have seen her."

"Proper folk are nothing but trouble."

"Nobody this side of the channel is proper," the man replied with a leer.

"Toph!" a voice bellowed. "You get your ass back here now!"

Toph laughed. "Whoops, gotta go. See you later at

the Blue?"

"Only if I don't have to pay your bail," Rath replied and handed over the hunk of cheese he'd bought before shoving Toph on his way. "Get going. The constable's wife, *honestly,* Toph."

Laughing, Toph darted in to kiss his cheek, then ran off just as a cluster of guards, led by a red-faced man with an enormous black mustache, drew close. The man bellowed and gave Rath a shove hard enough to send him sprawling on the muddy cobblestones, and then took off after Toph.

Picking himself up for the second time that morning, Rath brushed off what dirt he could as he once more headed for the bridge.

It was crowded, far more than was typical for the middle of the week, but the preliminary round of the Tournament of Losers was beginning soon. Hopefully Friar and the rest of the city's slush would be so busy terrorizing tourists that they'd leave the locals alone for a few months.

Rath pushed his way through a flock of fat swans who were bejeweled to the teeth: one quite literally; Rath did not understand noble fashion. He deftly relieved two of them of coin purses they were stupid enough to leave accessible. He shoved them away where he wouldn't lose them himself—and where a sharp-eyed guard wouldn't notice he had too many purses.

Across the bridge, he fell into the throng of an even greater crowd, mostly comprised of young, overeager fools who thought the Tournament of Losers offered a real chance at something better than their half-penny lives. Even walking as quickly as he could through the mess, Rath caught snatches of eagerly-spouted hopes and dreams. *When I marry the prince, I'll buy my parents a proper house. Once I win the tournament, I'll*

11

see the whole village gets what it needs! I'll never have to worry about food and shelter again.

He went tumbling when a particularly rowdy group accidentally knocked into him. "Sorry!" one of the young women exclaimed, shoving back a strand of limp, red-brown hair that had fallen from her cap.

Rath grunted an acknowledgment, but didn't slow, though he did catch the eye of their tolerant, exhausted parents and share a look of commiseration. He could still remember being a boy excited that he would be of an age to participate in the Tournament, indignant at the way all the adults scathingly called it the Tournament of Losers when it deserved its proper name: the Tournament of Charlet.

So-called for Regent Charlet, who had saved the kingdom several centuries ago in the first years of Queen Bardol II. Between plague and civil war, the whole country had been falling apart. It had taken a stray peasant to rise up and set all to rights. A woman with whom the queen had fallen madly in love. Tradition had been established that every seventy-five years, at least one immediate member of the royal and noble families must marry a peasant to bring in fresh blood and new perspective that would keep them from falling into the same patterns and arrogance that had once nearly destroyed the kingdom.

The nobles had protested that simply letting anyone marry into their families would do more harm than good, and that certain traits and skills were necessary to properly fulfill the duties expected of them. The solution had been a tournament where candidates could prove their suitability. It had been named for Regent Charlet, who was responsible for the law and the devising of the tournament.

Over time, the tournament had devolved into a mess of fools competing in challenges for no damned reason, since the nobles had rapidly mastered the art of manipulating, bribing, and otherwise cheating. It was well known that the vast majority of the winners were always 'peasants' only in the barest, most laughable sense. From the stories Rath did remember, they were often extremely young children of merchants or shopkeeps, or more often, orphans then given to said merchants and shopkeeps, and trained up to the exact specifications of the nobles in question. No *real* commoner had won the past five tournaments, and there had only been nine tournaments total so far. This would be the tenth, and some said the last, that the nobles were pushing harder and harder to do away with the idiotic matter for the 'good of everyone'.

Thank the Fates he'd left all that nonsense behind and knew to avoid the whole bloody thing. Rath might not possess much sense, but he had enough.

Finally making it through the congestion at the heart of High City, he threaded through a bunch of small side streets until he reached a small building at the southeast side. It was a modest townhouse, respectable enough for High City, but only sufficiently so to live at its edges, three steps from tumbling back down to Low City. It was three stories, only leaned slightly against the house to the right of it, and always smelled fragrantly of the teashop on the first floor. So much nicer than living at the ass end of Butcher Street and all the lovely smells *that* came with.

To the right of the teashop was a coffeehouse, and to the left of it was a small spiceshop, giving the whole area the most wonderful aroma. It was the only part of visiting his mother that he ever enjoyed, other than, of course, visiting his mother. He ducked into the narrow alleyway between the tea and coffee shops, pitch black because the way the houses leaned against each other meant practically no light slipped through.

He rapped on the high gate, and a few minutes later it swung open. A wrinkled, harried-looking face peered at him through rheumy blue eyes. "You already?"

"Me already," Rath agreed. "She about?"

"Make it quick. We're a bit too busy for your nonsense." The man slammed the door in his face.

Rath leaned against the stone wall that wrapped around the small courtyard behind the house and lit a cigarette. Sadly, he was down to his last two, and in light of recent circumstances, would not be buying more anytime soon. Unless the purses he'd snitched proved promising.

Pick-pocketing wasn't something he favored. It was often not worth the trouble, and these days, the punishment was a hundred times worse than the crime. He also just plain didn't like stealing, though it was too often necessary for people just trying to survive another day.

He pulled the purses out and tipped the contents into his hands. One held a shilling and two pennies. The second held two shillings and five pennies. All told, three shillings and seven pennies. That was enough money to keep him well for some time. But it was fourteen slick and twenty-two shillings short of what he needed to pay off Friar.

The gate creaked open, and he shoved it all away, mustering a smile he didn't feel as his mother, Alia Jakobson, stepped out into the alleyway, clutching a faded shawl about her shoulders, some of her dark, graying hair peeking out from the cap she wore.

Rath got all his looks from his mother—her gold-toned brown skin; loose, tumbling brown-black hair; pale brown eyes; and her height and bulk. When he'd been a boy, they'd lived closer to and worked at the docks, moving cargo with all the other day workers for a total of two pennies a day. He'd been so proud he'd been able to contribute half a penny extra to the family.

That his father was always quick to steal or bleed away on one foolish thing after another, until his mother finally threw him out and they moved to Butcher Street to live with his aunt and her husband. Then his aunt had died in a tavern brawl and his uncle had thrown them out. After that, they'd never lived anywhere very long, and often on the streets, until his mother found work in the teashop and Rath was old enough to work in the brothels.

Where he still worked from time to time when money was especially needed, though he preferred working at the docks, even if that had its own trials.

He finished his cigarette and dropped the stub to the ground, stamping it out as he asked, "Have you seen our least favorite piece of shit lately?"

Alia sighed. "He hasn't come by here for nearly a month, which I was enjoying. Do I want to know how bad it is?"

"Fifteen slick to Friar."

She swore as only ten years working the docks could teach a person. "I can't 'borrow' that kind of money from the shop, and even if I could, we'd never replace it before it was missed."

"I didn't come here to get the funds from you, just to figure out where that goat-faced spawn of a leech is hiding."

"I don't know, fortunately or unfortunately," she replied. "If I had to guess, I'd say the Old Gates. Nobody goes there unless getting their throat slit is the best option they've got."

Rath made a face, but mostly of resignation, because she was probably right. "Well, that will be fun." He leaned in to kiss her cheek, dug out two of the shillings from the purses he'd stolen. "Here, you may as well have these. It's not enough to make a difference to me, and Fates know what will happen to it if I keep it. Be well."

"Be careful," she said, patting his cheek and fussing with a strand of hair. "Give him a sound clocking from me."

"The first hit is always yours." He kissed her fingers, then lit a new cigarette and left as quickly as he'd come. Getting back across the city and the bridge was even more difficult than it had been the first time. As the day wore on the crowds would just get worse, with people coming from all over Dennarm on the futile hope they'd be one of the lucky few to marry into a wealthy family and make all their problems go away.

By the time he finally reached Low City again, Rath was hungry, cranky, and just waiting for an excuse to punch somebody. Except getting into a fight would make him too beat up and ugly to get any clients, and if he was going to come up with any slick at all, it was going to be pulling a few nights for Trinira.

But even that, if he was damned lucky, would only bring in about three marks. That was a long way from fifteen, but his best hope was that if he could scrape together at least a third, then Friar would give him time to earn the rest.

Of course, that hope rested entirely on the *reason* Friar was demanding fifteen slick right now, and Rath had yet to hear that reason.

He bought bread and pickles from another vendor, then started working his way back through Low City. Fates, his legs were going to be falling off by the end of the day.

The Low City was divided into four rough, unevenly-sized districts: docks, shops, propers, and guards. The docks and shops were the largest districts, where most everyone worked and lived. The propers were those merchants and a few others wealthy enough to live close to the bridges, so near to being on the other side of them that reaching that goal was a constant torment. The last section, the guards, was comprised of the city guard, some of the royal military who stayed there for the sake of convenience, and various mercenary bands as they came and went. They were the only ones permitted use of the guard bridge.

Rath walked steadily through the mazelike warrens of the shop district until he reached Honey Street, where all the brothels were located. Colorful, often garish signs hung from most of the buildings on the road, the colors indicating the flavors of the establishment.

He stopped in front of one that was painted with seven vertical bands of different colors crossed along the bottom by white, black, and gray bands. It signaled the house was willing to do pretty much anything and everything. There were other, informal indicators that it wouldn't do anything illegal—children, unwilling people, to name two. Houses that catered to such despicable clientele usually didn't last long, and the ones determined to stick around were extremely discreet and usually operated elsewhere in the city. But usually didn't mean always, so brothels were constantly forced to make it clear some lines would not be crossed.

His rap on the door was quickly answered, and by the lady of the house herself. By night, Mistress Trinira was beautiful enough to rival the Fates themselves, but by day, she preferred to keep to plain and simple, more interested in the bookkeeping and the cleaning than in looking decadent enough to make people loose with their coin.

She wore plain brown breeches and a blue tunic over a linen shirt, her long, long hair loosely piled atop her head, and spectacles perched on her nose. Her dark skin was smattered with freckles she'd never tolerate a customer seeing, and she had a cigarillo clenched in her teeth. "Good morning there, love. Didn't expect you to be coming around today. Thought you'd be picking up extra work at the docks." She leaned again the door frame and crossed her arms over her flat chest. "What are you doing all the way over here?"

"My plans for today were changed." Rath made a face.

She quirked one delicate, brown-red brow. "By who?"

"You don't want to know."

"You should dump your father's body in the harbor, or sell it to those cadaver lovers on Tanning Row. You'd make enough money to cover his debts with plenty to spare to spoil yourself. It's not like anyone would miss him."

"One of these days I might just, but right now it's still not worth the risk of being hauled to jail. I hate to bother you—"

She cut him off with a flap of her hand. "There's always work for a man of your skills, Rath. Especially with all these out-of-towners. Can you start early?"

"That shouldn't be a problem. I've got to track down my father and beat some answers out of him, but after that, my day is wide open. Anything special I should prepare for?"

"You up for group work?" she asked.

Rath shrugged. "Why not? Though don't they usually prefer the younger ones for that? I'm a bit long in the tooth to be the toy of a half-drunk group of horny nobles."

"No, this is a bit more refined group, and they want someone who knows what they're doing. I had Stripling in mind, but I haven't seen him in three days. Probably floating in cloud powder and bad gin by now, the stupid fool. Come around about four. We'll get you warmed up and then off to the noble lot around eight. Even taking the house percentage, that should square you away."

"Let's hope," Rath muttered, then leaned down to kiss her cheek. "Thanks, Trin. I'd be lost without you."

"Get along, then," she said, but smiled before sticking the cigarillo back in her mouth and closing the door.

Rath was already exhausted thinking about the night in front of him. At least three hours of letting a group of people fuck him. He hadn't done that in at least four years. The last adventurous night he'd had was a pair of twins who'd paid him well both for his talents and his ability to keep his mouth shut.

Anything was better than dead. And speaking of dead, it was time to go find his damned father.

It took another hour and a half of walking and asking questions, but he did finally locate the worthless pisspot, holed up in a moldy, rank-smelling tavern at the ass end of the docks known as the Old Gates, since it was once where all people entering from ships passed into the city. The sea gates had long ago been moved to the north end of the harbor district, and over the decades, the old location had turned into the sort of place even rats were loath to go.

He stepped into the tavern, grimacing at the smell, and skimmed the dingy, smoky place for a familiar face. He and his father saw each other at just the same time. His father stood, tried to bolt, and Rath stormed across the room and lunged at him.

"You scum-licking bastard!" Rath snarled, grabbing him by the back of his tunic. He yanked him close and then slammed the bastard's face into the bar. Leaving a penny to cover the tab, not bothering to give a damn about adding scratches and dents to a pub that was already covered in them, Rath hauled his father outside and threw him to the ground.

Planting a boot on his chest and pressing firmly, Rath said, "Tell me why the fuck I owe Friar fifteen slick, or I swear to the Fates, I will earn the money by selling your corpse."

"Get your boot—"

"Talk and I won't break your ribs."

Face turning red, his father snarled, "I'm your father. This isn't how you treat—"

"Do you really want to have this discussion, you putrid pile of dog puke?" Rath asked. "Because I bet my list about how people should treat their spouses and children is a lot longer than yours on how a child should treat their parents. Now tell me, or I will kick you in your balls and leave you wailing in the street like a drunk heretic." He pressed his boot down harder when it looked like a protest was forthcoming.

When his father started flapping his arms to signal a need to breathe, Rath finally eased some of the pressure. "Talk."

"I accidentally killed his best griffon."

"Fates—" Rath drew his boot back before he gave in to an urge to break the damned fool's ribs after all. "How in the names of the Fates do you accidentally kill a griffon?"

"It looked like it could use a drink," his father mumbled. "I gave it some gin."

"Spirits are *poison* to griffons, you hole-ridden sack of spoiled grain!" Rath wanted to *scream*. The dirty pit fights were where Friar made a goodly amount of his money, mostly from the brat nobles who liked nothing better than to slink into Low City and act like they were living dangerously by betting on which animal would kill the other first while gorging themselves on liquor and food that everyone in Low City could only dream about.

And his idiot fucking father had killed one of Friar's most lucrative assets, and no matter how much time passed, everybody still expected Rath to clean up his father's messes. "If I wind up floating in the harbor because of this, I swear to the Fates you'll fall first."

Spinning away, he made his way quickly back to the shop district and through the busy streets all the way to Butcher Street, where he rented a little attic room from Robert and Anta, a married couple who made and sold sausages. He waved to Anta as he passed by the yard and up the backstairs into the house, climbing the creaky old steps up to his hovel of a room.

It wasn't much, but he'd gotten it after twenty years of living in other people's spaces and occasionally on the street. No leaking roof, no other people he had to share with. All he had to deal with was the noise and the smell, and who cared about that?

Not him, not really.

He closed up the only window in the place to muffle some of the din, pulled off his boots and set them by the door, and hid his money in a secret cubby in the wall. Then, stripping off his clothes and hanging them up on hooks in the far corner, he crawled into his little bed to get some rest before he faced the long night ahead.

DESPERATE MEASURES

Rath woke up sore and still exhausted. He could hear the cry of vendors and shopkeeps outside, the bustle of shoppers, which meant it was well into morning. He groaned as he sat up, wincing at every ache and pain that made itself known.

Last night hadn't been bad as such things went, but he was in no hurry to repeat the venture. At least the group of five lords and ladies had been so pleased they'd left him a full mark tip in addition to the two marks they paid to the house for his services. That was two marks in total for him—a year's worth of wages in one night.

Whoring didn't usually bring in money that good, but between the group service and the fact they were from out of town... Well, one of the reasons he'd become a whore was the money. If not for his father, he'd have been living a lot better than he did.

So two marks down, thirteen to go. If he got another couple of good nights in the brothel, he'd be sure to pull in another mark, possibly two if the Fates would just once show him favor. Add in some purse lifting and turning a few tricks in the streets, and he might be able to pull together five marks. That would hopefully be enough to convince Friar to feel like being generous and give him more time to come up with the rest.

He finally climbed out of bed and walked stiffly across the room to the wash tub someone had been kind enough to leave. The water was warm, not hot, but he wasn't picky. Scrubbing away the mess left by his night, he rubbed a salve into the worst of his bruises and other sore spots. Pulling open the wardrobe, he pulled out the clothes he'd stowed there. He paused as he pulled on his jacket, took it off again, and looked at the worn elbow. Smiled when he saw someone had patched it for him. Looking again, he saw that someone in the brothel had, in fact, cleaned and repaired all his clothes. Probably the cleaning staff, they'd always been kind to him when he'd worked there.

Somewhat cheered about the day ahead, he pulled his jacket back on, ran a comb through his hair, and tucked away the mark his clients had left him as he hastened down to the kitchen by way of the back stairs. "Good morning!" he greeted Bettina, the house cook.

She didn't leave the pot she was stirring, but did look up briefly to smile at him. "There's food on the table for ye."

"You're the best." He sat at the nearest bench and quickly wolfed down the plate of bread with butter and honey, left over bits of cheese, even some slices of tart apple. Someone thunked a mug of ale down in front of him, and he looked up at a smiling Trinira. "Morning."

"Morning, handsome. You must have done a lot right because I rarely get personal thanks from that sort. They paid their balance without even a breath of hesitation." She slid his earnings across the table. He picked them up and tucked them away with his other mark. "You ever want steady work here again, you know it's yours. Coming back tonight?"

He nodded, gulped down the ale. "Yes, since you're so willing. I appreciate it, Trin."

She scoffed at him and drank her own ale. "So I think I might know a way you could earn ten marks, either today or tomorrow, depending."

"I doubt I'm physically capable of something that

would earn that much money in two days. I barely made it through all of last night."

Laughing, Trinira playfully slapped his arm. "I think you're underestimating yourself. Lucky for you, though, I wasn't talking about sex when I said I had an idea. I was talking about the Tournament of Losers."

He paused with a last bit of apple halfway to his mouth. "Fates, no. You can't be serious. I want no part of that stupid thing."

"Serious as a priest on prayer day," Trin drawled. "Think about it, darling. You could get through the elimination round easy enough, which puts you in the second round. Everyone who makes it to the second round is given ten marks to cover living expenses while they're competing and unable to work."

Rath opened his mouth, closed it again, then finally ate the bit of apple. "I think you're overestimating my skills, and the first bout of the elimination round is a melee, which is as much luck as skill. I could get my head caved in and come away with nothing but more debts I can't cover."

She shrugged. "If you don't try, you'll never get the money in time, and word on the street is that Friar is out for blood and not feeling inclined toward mercy."

"I see," Rath said and swore softly before finishing off the last few bites of his meal. There went any hope of convincing Friar to give him more time. Ugh, he was going to kill his father three times over for forcing him to get involved in something as stupid as the tournament. "Guess I'd better get to work, then."

Trin stood up with him, caught his arm. "Rath, I don't want you to come to a bad end, especially at Friar's hand, because your father is a fool. Try the tournament; I still think you'd be fine. That's ten slick, and I'll see to it you've got the remaining balance. You can pay me back at easier length. I know you're good for it."

Good to repay three slick, but not thirteen. But Rath couldn't really resent that, given how quickly he lost money because of his father. "I'll do my best not to need that. Guess I'd better give that stupid tournament a try." He groaned at the thought. "I think I'd rather just do group work for a week straight. I swear that would be less exhausting and painful. Not to mention less humiliating."

"Only you would think being a fuck toy is less humiliating than trying to marry into a better life." Trin shook her head. "Get the money and get out. It won't cost you more than a day, two at the most."

Rath sighed, but nodded. "Thanks for all your help, Trin." He kissed her cheek, then left out the back door, slipping through various rank-smelling alleyways until he came out on Baker's Row, where he could cut more easily up to the bridges, taking smaller roads that wouldn't be congested with visitors.

All the while, he tried to come up with some other means—any other means—that did not entail entering the stupid Tournament of Losers. Not that it really mattered in the end, because as Trin had said, it would only cost him an afternoon or two.

But it was the principle of the matter. The tournament was a bard's song, fool's gold. Rath might not have much sense, but he had enough to avoid participating in a spectacle put on for the masses to abide by the letter of the law. Like every other time before, the nobles had probably long ago selected and groomed suitable candidates. If the nobles hadn't already started cheating, they would soon, beginning with bribing tournament officials to ensure their pre-selected candidates made it through the preliminaries, or to learn ahead of time what the challenges would be. If their candidates failed anyway, there would also be bribes to fix that. Cheating wasn't hard, merely expensive.

He was going to be harangued endlessly by everyone who knew him, but there was no help for it. His only other option for getting that kind of money that fast was providing cadavers to the strange trio that was always happy to pay generously for bodies and ask no questions about where they came from. What they did with the bodies, nobody had ever been brave enough to ask.

Rath had once helped a friend take his father's body to them after the man had dropped from too much booze and fighting. One of the most miserable nights of his life, though not as bad as it had been for his friend, who'd actually liked his father, but needed the money and was doing only what his father had ordered.

The horrible evening had earned Rath fifteen shillings, though. He hadn't needed to worry about money for three whole weeks. Then his father had turned up and ruined everything, but three weeks of peace was more than he usually got.

Giving up on finding alternate means of earning money fast, Rath tried to dredge up what he knew about the tournament. People had told him countless stories when he'd been young and stupid enough to be excited, to think he might be one of the lucky few to marry into a noble house, *or maybe, mama, I'll get to marry a prince or princess!*

He winced at the memory, tried to think of something to banish it again. Like all the stories people had told him when he was older about how stupid and pointless the tournament truly was. Or the rules. Those would be useful to remember if he was actually going to do this.

Rules, rules, rules. Thousands always showed up to compete, and it would take far too long to give that many the full gauntlet of challenges. So over the course of a couple of days, five back when the tournament had been more popular, competitors were whittled down in two rounds.

The first round was the melee, a mad free-for-all dash across a specially built 'battlefield'. All competitors were given flags before the melee started, and the goal was to keep those flags while stealing them from everyone else. The more flags captured, the more likely a competitor was to go on to the next round. There was a record set, for some ridiculous amount, but Rath no longer remembered it.

The second round was dueling, something like best of five or whatnot. He didn't remember that, either. Once, he'd had *everything* memorized. The number of marriage slots, all the titles, the different kinds of challenges and the keys to success for each, the records set for all of them, on and on and on he'd gone. So much energy wasted on something so stupid.

All he remembered now was that there were seventy-seven noble houses, plus the royal family, which meant seventy-eight marriage slots. Six duchies, seventeen earldoms, and fifty-four baronies. Approximately five thousand people, give or take a grand, would be showing up to compete for a chance. All but five hundred of them would be whittled out in the first two days, and that wasn't counting the ones who weren't approved for competition.

Because to participate at all, the competitor must be: Between the ages of twenty and forty. Have no trace of noble lineage for at least seven generations. Must not have family that won the previous tournament. No arrests within the last three years and absolutely no convictions of major crimes, which were rape, murder, grand theft, and arson.

That eliminated plenty, but still left a surplus of

options.

What the melee didn't take care of, the duels did, reducing the final number of contestants to five hundred. After that came the sorting round, where the five hundred were sorted into who would compete to marry the royal family, the dukes, the earls, and the barons. After that came the final round, months of absurd, arbitrary challenges meant to prove that the pathetic little peasants were fit to become hoity-toities.

Rath would much rather do anything else, but he'd faced worse. He could endure the stupid tournament long enough to earn ten slick.

"Raaaaath!"

He turned around as Toph came barreling at him, because Toph had somehow never learned to simply *walk* anywhere. He oofed when Toph slammed into him and hugged him tight. "Morning, Toph."

"Where have you *been?* I waited at the pub for you to show! All night!"

Rath groaned. "I'm sorry, Toph. I've been busy cleaning up my father's latest mess. Spent the whole night working at Trin's. I totally forgot."

Toph wrinkled his nose. "Your dad again? Haven't you put him in the harbor or sold his body yet?"

"Everyone keeps suggesting that second one. I'm somewhat alarmed about the company I keep."

"Like you're company to be going on about," Toph retorted cheerfully, linking their arms as they resumed walking. "So where you headed now? Got time for a pint?"

"Maybe later. I'm, uh—" Rath wrinkled his face, then sighed. "I'm still ten slick short."

"Holy Fates!" Toph said. "What in the name of Belna's balls did he do this time?"

Heaving another sigh, Rath told him. By the end, poor Toph looked so stressed on his behalf, Rath would have bought him a drink if he hadn't needed to focus on what he was doing. "Come on, stand in line with me, so I don't go mad or panic and dash at the last moment."

Toph shrugged. "I've never know you to dash from anything, but I've got nothing else to do until tonight. Got work at Wynri's place."

"Since when are you the pain sort?"

"Pain, no, but what's a little silk rope here and there? Oh, hang on, I'm hungry. You want something?"

Rath shook his head, laughing softly. "I never refuse food, but since when do you have money? Steal that from the constable, along with his wife's affections?"

"That woman only loves herself and has no interest in loving anyone else—it's my favorite thing about her," Toph said, then darted over to a nearby street vendor to cheerfully haggle for his lunch. He returned a few minutes later with steaming pies that smelled of chicken and gravy and good vegetables. "As to the coin," he said, when Rath gave him a suspicious look. "The others bet I'd end the night in the stocks and they'd have to come pay the bailiff to let me out in the morning. But I stayed the whole night free as a rat, and they all had to pay up."

Rath gave his head a playful shove. "The constable is still going to have your nethers for a coin purse when he finds you."

"Che," Toph said and wolfed down several bites of his pie, wiping his mouth with the back of his hand before adding, "He's busy with all the out of town rabble, and by the time he can go back to dealing with local rabble, he'll be mad at the most recent stranger in his bed. He'll have forgotten all about me." A quick grin. "Again."

"You're playing with Fate," Rath replied. "Be careful or you'll wind up in a noose."

"I will, I will," Toph replied easily. He finished his pie and pulled out a tattered kerchief from one of his jacket pockets to clean his face and hands.

Rath finished his own and was clean and ready as they stepped onto the common bridge, threading carefully through the crush. He would have loved a chance to lift a few purses, but the congestion made it too dangerous. Easy pickings, but if they got caught, there was nowhere to run.

When they were finally through, he resisted the urge to check his own coin. Nothing drew a thief's eye faster than being told precisely where the money was kept. "I can't wait for this to be over. I've walked more in the past two days than I have the past two *weeks*. What's a person got to do to be left to honest labor and a pint or two at the end of the day?"

"Kill your father and sell his body to—" Toph snickered when Rath clapped him upside the head.

"Stop talking about murder. It's ill-luck to do it so often, and I've had about all the bad luck I can take right now—and if I'm going to get ten slick for punching people, then I need all the good luck I can find," Rath said, then added with a mutter, "since divine intervention ain't likely."

Toph smiled, reaching out to squeeze his arm. "Come on, you'll do fine. I've seen the way you sling around grain sacks and move those barrels. You can clobber a few country idiots and take their flags without a sweat."

"Maybe," Rath replied, then their talking faded off as they reached the top of High City, where the pavilion and the royal castle were located.

The pavilion was teeming with people like fish in a barrel with most of the water sloshed out, and there was so much racket, Rath could barely hear himself think. He wasn't one for dashing, it was true, but right then, he was ready to start a new habit.

"What do the signs say? I don't know the marks." Toph asked in that small voice of his that rarely cropped up, since it was hard to make Toph feel insecure about anything. Rath had always loved and admired the trait. But Toph's inability to read, though it was something he shared with most of Low City, always upset him.

Rath squinted at the signs, but they were hard to read with the sun shining in his eyes, and his vision was not really the best at long distances. There were three signs lined up evenly across the pavilion, and only then did he notice the crush actually had some sense to it: enormous, bulging, writhing lines. The signs had letters and circles of colors beneath: red, blue, green from left to right. "Uh. The first one says 'ages 20-25', the second 'ages 26-30', and the last '31-40'." He winced, unable not to notice that line wasn't even half as long as the other two, and the first one was half again as long as the second.

Not surprising, really. The stupid tournament was a young person's folly. But it was humiliating all the same to see how glaringly out of place he was going to be. "You may want to wait for me here."

"How is that better than just staying with you? Come on. You're going to turn white if you keep thinking instead of doing."

"That doesn't make any sense," Rath groused, but let Toph drag him along. They pushed and shoved and swore their way through the crush until they at last reached the back of the line.

"Ho, Rath!" A chorus of men greeted congenially. Men he knew from the docks and his preferred pub. "Did you get dragged into this stupid bet, too?"

"What bet? No, you know I don't gamble. It's bad fate for my family."

"You're so superstitious for such a cynical git," said one of the men, black as night, thin and scraggly as a winter tree. But that slender frame had surprising strength; Rath had seen Mick put men thrice his size down with a single blow. "No, no, some fellas at the Crow said we wouldn't last five minutes in the melee. There's a pot. Whoever gets the most flags wins it."

"Whatcha doing here, then, Rath?" asked another man, as large as the first man was skinny, with snow-pale skin and ale-yellow hair.

Rath grinned. "What do you think, Coor? Hiding from your husband."

The four men all laughed, and Coor clapped him on the back. "As if my man would give you the time of day. He prefers men that don't tower over him like a damned tree."

"Come on, Rath, it's not like you to care about this sort of thing. Did Toph here dare you to sign up?"

"No, but I should have thought of that!" Toph said brightly, then yelped when Rath jabbed him in the ribs.

Rath poked him again, then turned to the others. "No, just my father." They all grumbled and commiserated and offered to help beat him up, but Rath waved them all off. "What's the pot, so I know how many pints one of you will be buying me?"

That got him more laughter, and from there they were happy to catch him up on the gossip he'd missed the past several days while he'd been busy working at the docks and been too damned tired to do much more than fall into bed. His evening with the pretty man he'd had to leave behind had been the first time he'd had fun in more than a week.

By the time it was finally his turn at the registration table, Rath was almost in a good mood.

"Name, age, address," the clerk, dressed in royal blue and purple livery, demanded curtly.

Rath winced slightly. "Rathatayen Jakobson, thirty-three, Robert's sausage shop."

The clerk looked up, seemed to freeze momentarily before recovering and once more just looking bored and tired. "Occupation?"

"Free laborer."

"Lab—" the clerk broke off and hastily ducked his head to jot it down.

Ah, now Rath got it. The man had been a client at Trin's probably, or mayhap one Rath had picked up on the street. "Yeah, laborer. Is that a problem?"

"No," the clerk said, barely audible. He looked up. "I just—"

"What? Thought I couldn't be something other than a whore? What's wrong with being a whore, anyway?"

The clerk's mouth pinched. "I was just expecting you to say something else, that's all."

Rath scoffed, but let it drop. Picking a fight with a harried clerk would just get him arrested for being a nuisance, and then he'd have to hand over what little coin he had to post his bail and bribe the bailiff into not filing the arrest. "Any other questions?"

"Are you trained in any martial arts?"

"Only the six months everyone does."

"Can you read and write?"

"The law says that doesn't matter," Rath said.

The clerk glared at him. "It's not a qualification; it's just general information."

"The law says it doesn't matter, so I'm not saying."

"If you don't say, you don't compete. It's not required, but we do need to know in order to adjust the challenges accordingly."

Rath bit back a curse. "Yes, I can read and write."

The clerk resumed writing. "Any illnesses, injuries, or other possible impediments that should be accounted for in your challenges?"

"No."

"Fine. Read and sign here. If you need anything read to you, just say."

Rath picked up the heavy piece of paper and read it all the way through, frowning at some of the longer words, but puzzling them out after a bit from context. When he was done, and as satisfied as he was going to get, he laid it back down, took the quill the clerk still held out, and quickly scratched his name at the bottom.

The clerk set the paper aside to dry and handed Rath a small wooden chip painted bright red and marked with what seemed to be the head of a cat in white. "You're in the second melee. Show up this afternoon at half past the second hour at the fairgrounds. Gather under the blue tent. Someone will explain the rules and distribute the flags. If you fail to show, you are automatically disqualified. You can't compete without that chip, so don't lose it."

Nodding, Rath tucked the chip away and made his escape. "I need a damned drink," he said when he and Toph were finally away from the pavilion.

"I'm happy to buy you two, even," Toph said, and they made their way back to the Low City where the ale was both good and cheap.

Two ales wound up closer to five. Possibly six. But it was a few hours where Rath could pretend that his life wasn't wholly dependent on surviving a melee and several duels.

When the midday bells tolled, however, there was no longer any avoiding his fate. He drained the dregs of his latest ale, threw down a farthing to help cover any stray costs, and clapped Toph on the back. "I'm off to get my ass pounded in a damned unpleasant way. I'll see you sorry lot later tonight, or tomorrow."

Toph kissed his cheek and the others at the table lifted their tankards in farewell, calling out cheerful assurance he'd be fine and best of luck.

Salvare was the royal city, crown of Dennarm, situated at the northeast corner of the country and right up against the sea. Rath only knew that because of his years working the docks, and hiding away in the office of a kindly clerk when he was too young, but his mother didn't want to leave him at home. It was how he'd first started learning to read and write. One of the other reasons he'd taken up whoring was that brothels were willing to teach reading and writing, among other things, in order to offer additional costly services to their customers.

Outside the high city walls were the fairgrounds, built back during the first tournament, repurposed from the old military practice grounds that had been abandoned long ago in favor of new yards and quarters within the walls. The fairgrounds were tucked in a little hollow formed by the city walls, the cliffs that backed the city, and the river that cut it in half. The grounds had burned down two and a half times since they were first built, mostly due to drunken carelessness combined with too many overexcited idiots.

Between tournaments, they were used for various holiday revelries and by the military once, sometimes twice, a year to do their foolish jousting thing which mostly involved drinking and knocking each other over. The rest of the time High City's finest—stupidest—youths did their best to imitate the jousts, with a good deal more alcohol and falling off horses involved.

Rath passed through the enormous southern gates and joined the milling throng headed down the small side road that split off from the main and led to the fairgrounds, over a wide, sturdy bridge that wasn't quite as elegant as the city bridges, built simply to be serviceable.

The smell of roasting meat, sausages dripping fat and pies near to bursting with tender fowl, made his stomach growl. Living above a sausage shop gave him more chance at meat than most, but even then, it was still rare he got any. The pie Toph had bought him earlier was the first bit of meat he'd had in ages.

"Ho, there, rapscallion," cried a familiar voice.

Rath stopped and looked around, brows lifting in surprise as he saw the pretty man he'd fucked the other night and had been forced to abandon in the morning thanks to Friar. High City brats weren't normally worth the trouble unless he was getting paid, but this one… Damn, what was his name? He'd been worth the trouble. "Ho, there, High City."

The man's grin widened as he caught up to Rath. He was a few fingers taller than Rath, which was somewhat unusual, but had none of Rath's heft or width. "Off to see the melee? You seemed so scathing of the tournament, I'd have bet ten crowns you wouldn't go near the fairgrounds while it was on." He flicked his head, throwing the long mass of heavy braids over his shoulder. They were unornamented, which was unusual, as elaborate hair and face ornamentation were all the fashion up High City way. Rare to see a High City who didn't have their hair painted red and blue with jewels and birds pinned in it.

"That's a fortune you'd lose, as I'm to be *in* the damned melee, now," Rath replied.

"Oh?" The man's steps faltered for a moment, eyes widening briefly. "How did that come about?"

"It's related to that matter that took me from bed the other morning."

"I see." His brow furrowed. "No, I rather don't. What does this have to do with that?"

Rath shook his head. "It's a boring tale, I promise. I take it you've come to spectate, pretty boy?" He cocked his head, eying the man thoughtfully. "Seeing what your marriage prospects are going to be, maybe?"

The man made a face. "Maybe."

"How very spoiled brat of you to go about breaking rules just to satisfy curiosity."

"Wouldn't you? Anyway I'm hardly doing any harm this early on," the man replied, his easy grin returning. "Though speaking of things I shouldn't do, I have shamefully forgotten your name."

Rath laughed. "Well I don't recall yours either, so we'll call it even. Most call me Rath. My whole name is a mouthful and not worth knowing."

"That's not true, or I wouldn't be trying to learn it a second time. My name's Tress."

"Well met, Tress."

"Well met, Rath." Tress's smile softened, taking on flirtatious tones. "What are you doing after the melee?"

"Recovering," Rath replied. "If I'm even standing at the end of it, I'll be impressed."

Tress sighed. "Fair enough, I suppose. What team are you part of?"

"Team?"

"What does your token have on it?"

"Oh." Rath dug out the chip he'd shoved into his coin purse (that never held anything as valuable as money—only idiots kept their coin where anyone else could get it). "A cat, whatever that means."

Tress snickered. "Cat. That's a lion's head."

"What in the Fates is a lion?"

"A cat bigger than a man that hunts… mm, deer and such, in grasslands far, far away from here."

"So it *is* the head of a cat."

"Well, yes, but like calling a wolf a dog."

"Whatever," Rath replied, skin flushing hot as he shoved the token away. He didn't know what a lion was; who cared?

Tress's smile collapsed. "I'm sorry, I didn't—"

"Forget it," Rath snapped, grateful that they'd reached the bustling fairgrounds. "I have to be off to the blue tent or some such. If I'm not dead or unconscious afterward, you're welcome to buy me a pint or two."

Smile returning, Tress said, "Looks like you've had plenty of those already."

"Why would anyone do this sober?" Rath muttered. Especially given how damned sore he was from a long day of walking, followed by a night of fucking, followed by more walking. Fates, he just wanted to sleep for a couple of days.

"I certainly wouldn't," Tress said. He snagged Rath's wrist and drew him to a halt. Lifting Rath's hand, he pressed something into it, then bent and pressed a light kiss to each of Rath's cheeks. "A token and a kiss for luck. Fates See your victory."

He was gone before Rath could form a reply. Frowning, he opened his hand and stared at the object: a small wooden charm, the type meant to be affixed to clothes or made into an earring or pendant, bought from temples for three a farthing. Prayer charms, meant to imbue the bearer with various and sundry blessings and keep the temples in funds. Tress had given him a charm of fortune.

Why had Tress been carrying it around? He couldn't have known he'd meet Rath again, and even if he had, why buy such a silly thing for some Low City fuck? He must have bought them for something else and decided to give Rath one, maybe out of guilt or pity.

Shoving it into his coin purse, clutching his token, Rath headed for the bright blue tent at the far end of the grounds.

MELEE

Rath spat out blood and dodged the screaming woman coming at him, catching her soundly in the stomach as she passed him and stealing her single remaining flag as she fell to the ground. He shoved it into his jacket just as a pair of men came into view, both clutching weights that would add a nasty heft to their punches. They were also against the rules, but when had that ever stopped anyone?

He avoided one, but took a clip to the jaw from the other that sent him stumbling into someone behind him. That got him a rough kick and a flag lost—but sent him crashing into the first pair and knocking them all to the ground. Rath punched them both, kneed one in the groin, stole two flags apiece from both, and got out of there while they were still trying to figure out which way was up.

How much longer was this nightmare going to last?

He was down to two flags out of five himself, which meant he was probably going to be out of the fight soon, though hopefully he'd leave with enough flags to qualify him for the duels.

Though what he was going to duel *with* was a mystery. Common folk didn't learn martial skills the way the nobility did. They had six months rudimentary training and then were allowed to go back to their lives. High City folk had to learn far more—and spent a good deal of money doing it.

Rath knew the sharp end of the sword and where to

stick it, but only from required lessons taken back when he was fourteen. His skills with a knife were more suited to household chores than hurting people. If his fists weren't enough to get him through the first two rounds, then he was out of luck.

He dodged around a fellow roughly the size of a ship and with all the grace of a sinking ship. He'd just gotten into it with a woman who seemed to have soldierly training when the horns blew, making him start. Rath bolted away from the woman as quickly as he could manage, every single bone and muscle in his body hurting, and returned to the edge of the field.

A field that had started out a pristine stretch of swept earth was now littered with unconscious people, bits of torn clothes, and splashes of blood. One of the criers ordered them to form lines in front of the tables and be ready to have their flags counted. If they had no flags, they were to go to the table at the farthest end.

But that was not Rath's problem. When he finally reached the table, he dumped his collection of flags on it, then handed over the single one of his own he had remaining.

"Four lost, twenty-three gained," the clerk said. "Go stand beneath the blue tent."

Giving the flippant version of a soldier's salute, back of his hand facing out, fingers touched to his brow before flicking them sharply out, he spun away and stamped over to the blue tent. Where he promptly dropped to the ground and lowered his head to keep from throwing up. Maybe drinking five or six ales before getting into a massive brawl hadn't been the wisest choice. Fates grant him mercy, how was he supposed to work for Trin that night when he could barely move?

But that was a problem to deal with in a few more hours. Hopefully he would be free of the damned tournament soon and could get some rest before facing the long night ahead of him.

He looked up at the sound of a ruckus, saw a man bellowing and shouting, a clerk sprawled on the ground. Angry guards came up and dragged the man away. Wincing, Rath hauled himself to his feet and leaned carefully against one of the poles supporting the tent. "What's going on?"

"If I had to guess," said a rough, but pretty voice with an accent definitely not from the city, "I'd say he tried to cheat. Maybe bought the flags off those who only had one or two and obviously weren't going to make it."

Rath grunted. Smart, but not worth the risk. He turned to look at the speaker, a handsome woman with skin slightly darker than his own and reddish-brown hair that had been woven into a thick, heavy braid that stopped just past her neck. Definitely not from the city, because in the city, only nobles could afford to keep their hair long. For everyone else, hair kept long rapidly became filthy and vermin-infested. "See it worked well for him."

The woman shrugged. "Gotta be smart and careful, and anyone cheating in line is neither of those things." She held out a hand, palm up. Rath laid his own it; they curled their fingers together in a formal greeting that no one in the city bothered with ever. "Kelni of Rier Village."

"Rath Jakobson. So where is Rier?"

"Dead south of here, about six days on foot. Fishing village."

Rath grinned. "Is that why you smell like fish?"

"Shush your mouth, city boy. What excuses you smelling like a pub?"

"I was in one for three hours, and I'm a day laborer losing wages to get beat up for scraps of cloth," Rath replied.

Kelni laughed. "Fair enough. Going to retrieve my sisters after this and find a drink or three of my own. What's a good place to rent rooms that won't lose me every penny to my name?"

"Cart Street, seventh house on the left coming from the south end. It's got a red bird painted on the door. She lets room to folks with a recommendation. If you tell her I sent you, she'll let you stay. If she's already full up, she'll know a good place to send you. For food, try the Blue Minstrel. Good and cheap, they don't water the drinks overmuch, and the ale doesn't taste like piss."

She beamed at him, lightly touched his arm. "Thank you, you've been very kind."

Rath shrugged. "Plenty of others could have helped you just the same. Uh, looks like they're summoning us. Fates lead you to Fortune."

"May they lead you to the same, city boy." She winked and slipped away to join the crowd milling toward a beckoning crier.

When they'd all gathered around the crier, who was standing on a barrel and holding a sheet of paper, he cleared his throat and bellowed out, "If your name is called, go to the tables to receive your token for the duels. If your name is not called, you have been eliminated. Duelists are to report here tomorrow by after-prayer bell. Anyone who does not show up on time forfeits their place in the tournament."

Rath sighed as the crier started listing off names, not sure if he wanted to hear his or not, no matter how much he *needed* to hear it. He gritted his teeth as his bruises and scrapes and two days of over-exertion grew increasingly difficult to ignore. He might have to surrender to it and pop over to Vix's for a powder or two to get him through the night. Hopefully, Trin would let it slide. She knew how much he hated relying on such things. A good ale and the odd swig of gin was the most adventurous he cared to get.

He stirred, tried to pay attention, when he heard increased grumbling from the people around him. Rath looked where they were staring, at the group of people approaching the tables to receive their tokens. Ah. The future spouses, at least half of them. They were too clean and well-dressed to be true Low City or country folk, no matter how hard they worked at it. Commoners legally, but they had been trained up for noble life since birth, just like those they planned to marry, and they'd have every possible advantage in the tournament. Only the Fates knew how the tournament would really end, but it didn't take divine might to mark a posse of cheats and reckon the odds.

"Rathatayen Jakobson!" the crier bellowed.

Relief and disappointment rushed through him, along with the usual resignation as people sniggered at his name. Rath limped over to the tables to receive his token. He tucked it away in his coin purse. "So what do the duels entail, are we allowed to ask?"

"Fight to first blood, no weapons allowed," the clerk replied, smiling and brushing back a lock of bright blonde hair that had slipped free of the knot at the back of her head. "Can you read? We have a rule sheet you can look over, though I'm happy to tell you them."

"I can read," Rath said. "Rule sheet sounds easier for everyone."

"It's no trouble at all," she replied, but slid a small piece of paper across the table.

So much paper and ink. Rath was glad he wasn't the one having to fund the tournament, because the writing stuffs alone were a fortune. Rolling the paper up, he stuck that in his coin purse as well, then limped off slowly back to the city.

He had to stop several times to catch his breath and let the pain ebb. When he stumbled on the road, not even halfway back to the city, he could have cried. He was too old for this nonsense. He just wanted steady work and a good meal at the end of the day. Why was he stuck dealing with tournaments and whoring and his useless fucking father?

A hand fell on his shoulder, and before he could look up, someone had hauled him to his feet. Whatever he'd expected, it wasn't emerald-brilliant eyes filled with concern and kindness. "All right there, Rath?"

"Been better," Rath admitted. "Don't think I'm up to having an ale with you, High City, much as I'd have enjoyed it."

Tress rolled his eyes. "The ale can wait. Let's get you home."

"I can take care of myself. I don't need some High City brat—"

"Stuff it," Tress replied. "We have a term for people like you in High City."

"You have several terms, and I've heard them all," Rath muttered.

Tress opened his mouth, but then snapped it shut, a tight frown replacing his amusement.

"Oh, did I offend your delicate sensibilities, poppet?"

"Stuff it," Tress repeated. "No, I was mad about something else. Anyway, the term *I* was talking about is 'too proud to suffer life'. I guess that's a phrase, strictly speaking. The point stands."

Rath gave him a look as they started walking along. "I'm not even certain what the point is, that you hoity-toities use seven words when two will do? Because it's easier just to call me pig-headed."

"That doesn't sound nearly as mocking."

"Stuff it."

Tress laughed. "Do well in the melee?"

"I'm stuck with the duels, so I must have," Rath replied. "So tell me, fancy boy, why do they bother with all of this nonsense, waste all this time and money, when the candidates are already decided upon and we're obviously just going through the motions?"

"There's not as much cheating as you obviously think. As to why we still do the tournament, it's because of this thing called obeying the law. Changing a law like that is no easy matter. When the Tournament of Charlet was first established, Regent Charlet made damned good and sure it would stick, and she had friends aplenty, so they say, to help her. So it's stuck, and there are more than enough Traditionalists in seat to make sure it continues to stick, no matter how loud the opposition gets. It's actually pretty hard to successfully rig the tournament, and even the best of plans can be upset by a stray fisherman with more talent and determination than anyone expected."

Rath peered up at him, somewhat distracted despite himself by the handsome lines of Tress's face, the faintest hint of stubble, and the way he smelled like the warm, spiced tea that Rath only ever got at the Winter Peace festival when the temples handed it out free for a day as part of their duties to the poor. Free tea and free food: that was all Rath cared about. "You seem to know a lot, but I guess for nobles there's as much to be lost as we have to gain."

"Depends on who you ask," Tress said moodily.

The levity that had been reviving died again. "I'm asking *you,* halfwit. You seem to care too much for someone not directly affected by the matter. Though I suppose it could be a sibling on the chopping block."

"Nope, I've got two siblings already married, and one gone off to priestly things. I've always been intended as the tournament prize. I *want* to be the tournament prize, though I'm in no hurry to be married to a stranger I might wind up hating or who hates me, though there are ways to deal with that should it happen." He smiled. "I'd tell you my house, but that would be cheating."

"I'm fairly certain just talking to me, especially about the tournament, is cheating."

"Not if you don't know who I am. I could be lying," Tress replied. "Anyway, it'll only count if I get caught."

Rath rolled his eyes. "Spoken like a true High City. Are we done walking yet?"

Tress laughed and altered their course, helped Rath over to a low bit of wall that framed the yard behind the gatehouse. "We can take a break. I don't know where you live, anyway."

"Butcher Street," Rath said and slumped against him, unable to stay upright. Everything *hurt.* "I may as well give up and turn myself in to Friar now."

"You're doing all this because of a friar?"

Rath snorted and sat up enough to give him a look. "Not *a* friar, *the* Friar." He sighed when Tress just gave him a baffled look. "He runs the pit fights and is in charge of most of the smuggling around here, a lot of the gambling pits, too."

"Oh, right."

Rath gave him an even more scathing look.

Tress smiled sheepishly. "All right, all right. I've never heard of him. I honestly didn't know there was one person in charge of that sort of thing. I, uh, don't leave the house much. My eldest brother says if it wasn't for sex, I'd never get my nose out of a book."

"One of that sort, eh?" Rath smiled at the thought, and a memory flickered through his mind. "It was a book that made me start talking to you."

Tress's face lit up. "You remember. Yes, it was a book that provoked conversation. You wanted to know how snotty or idiotic I could possibly be that I'd bring a book to a bar."

"You said it was a book of..." Rath frowned, trying to recall the ridiculous word Tress had used. "Some stupidly fancy word for sex stories."

"Erotic," Tress replied, mouth curving in a smile that Rath definitely remembered, and if he hadn't felt like he'd been run over by the shit-collector's cart, he might have been up to seeing if he could get a repeat. "It was a volume of erotic stories. You wanted to know why in the Fates I'd bother to read about sex when a pretty boy like me could be having it."

Rath rolled his eyes. "I remember where the night went after that. Pathetic, I'm not usually that easy when it comes to your sort."

"I should be offended at all the scathing ways you can say things like *High City* and *your sort* and *hoity-toity*, but it's oddly appealing, like the burn of good whiskey. There's also the way it makes me stare at your mouth."

"Go dunk your head," Rath said. "I've heard better from paying cust—" He broke off, pleasure draining away, replaced by dread. *Stupid.*

But instead of pulling away or getting angry or any of the other unpleasant things that High City people did when they learned he was a whore, Tress just laughed. "I refuse to believe that I give worse compliments than paying customers. For one, they're paying, which means they don't even mean it."

"And you're the first sincere nob to ever exist? I'm a whore, not a fool. I thought you were taking me home."

"You were tired and wanted a rest."

Rath ignored that and stood up, immediately regretting it, but there was little choice. He needed to rest before work that night, or the damned afternoon would have been a waste. Tress pulled one of Rath's arms across his shoulders, got his own arm around Rath's waist, and they resumed walking.

After a few minutes, he asked, "Do you even know where Butcher Street is?"

"I've memorized a city map, so yes," Tress said.

Rath knew that tone. "How many times have you gotten lost?"

"Dunk your head," Tress muttered. "If I could find a bit of you that wasn't banged up, I'd give you a solid pinch."

Rath laughed, even though doing so hurt. "Turn left here. Oh, no, a pinching! Now you've scared me into respecting my betters should I ever come across them."

"Hahaha, never heard that in Low City before. Be quiet like a good invalid. Left here, are you sure?"

"Do I look like a High City boy to you? Yes, left here. There was a sewer travesty last year, and they had to tear up the whole place. Smoke Street cuts right through Cobbler Row, which will take us to Butcher Street."

Tress huffed. "Somebody needs to update the maps, especially if that change has been in place for a year! There's no excuse for such slovenly practice—" He broke off when Rath laughed, but petulantly added, "They should update the maps."

"Poor delicate nob. Pretty maps out of date, how is he to learn the city if he doesn't have an accurate map to stare at for hours on end?"

"You sound like my father and brother, and that is not at all how I want to regard you," Tress replied, still sounding petulant. They drew to a halt as they reached a cross street. "So… right here?"

"Good guess, High City. Right and continue on until you see the shop with the blue door, then we turn left."

"As you command."

They resumed walking, lapsing into a silence that was far too comfortable for Rath's liking. Especially when he was already getting along with Tress as easily as he would Toph or one of the other fellows. But that had been what drew him the other night, why he'd decided to play with a High City when normally he avoided that lot harder than he avoided the city guard. Tress was… affable, easy, and genuinely sweet. The sort of idiot who read a book in a pub and didn't care what others thought of him for it.

Hopefully, after he dropped Rath off, he would have appeased his desire to do a good deed for the poor and go on his merry way. Unless he was hoping for another go in the bedroom, but Rath was barely going to be capable of doing that for Trin in a few hours.

Whatever. Nobles always got bored of slumming it eventually. Tress would totter off from boredom or the need to chase something newer and shinier.

"We're here. I thought you'd look more excited."

"I'm not going to give you a compliment. You probably get enough of those," Rath retorted. "You don't need to help me up the stairs; I'll never live that down."

"Very well, I know an order when I hear it." Tress swept him a bow fit for a prince.

Rath gave him a shove, or as much of one as he could manage. "Go away. People are staring."

"I'll see you later tonight," Tress replied and winked before spinning away like a dancer. Or maybe a drunk. He hummed as he walked along the street. The idiot was going to get his boots and coin purse stolen.

Rath watched him until he was out of sight, then trudged into the shop and slowly, painfully made his way all the way up the stairs.

Pulling off his clothes, adding 'laundry' to his

mental list of things he really needed to do once Friar was taken care of, he tumbled into his bed. Moaned as the rough landing jarred every last pain and doubled the agony. He closed his eyes, tried to count to lull his mind into sleep.

A soft knock at the door made him whimper. "Come in." He hoped it wasn't Robert asking about rent, because he still had a week to pay it, and he hadn't been late the past seven times. The man could bugger off.

But it was only Anta. She looked around his room with a gentle shake of her head, giving him one of those peculiar smiles that was affectionate and gently reprimanding all at once. "Honestly, Rath, what are you doing getting involved in that tournament? Thought you had more sense."

"Believe me, I do, and I'm not in it by choice. Is something wrong? I'll have rent when it's—"

"Shush now, I didn't come to pester you about that," she said and set down a small pitcher and glass, followed by three twists of paper. Medicine. "A boy came by, said these were for you, from your favorite pretty idiot."

"That nob," Rath muttered, then hastily said, "sorry," when Anta gave him a warning look for his language. The whole street had heard her butcher her husband like one of his pigs when he got to swearing too much. Listening to her, he could see why she thought it unnecessary. A customer spewing insults wasn't half as vulgar or creative as Anta could get when she was riled. When she wasn't riled, she was sweeter than fresh honey. Somehow, that just made her more frightening. "Thanks for bringing it up. I don't need more than one, though, if you want the other two." She hesitated. The powders were expensive, so Anta didn't get them often, though they were one of the few things that could help her husband's back, which was pretty much constantly in pain. Rath feebly flapped a hand. "Go on. You know I don't use the stuff much. What would I do with it all?"

"Well, bless, Rath. I'll see something is adjusted in the rent, eh? He brought you the fine stuff. Surprised that boy didn't just vanish with it. Take it and get some rest. Come down to the kitchen before you go out tonight and I'll have supper for ya."

"Thanks, Anta." When she'd gone, he managed to sit up enough to pour himself some water and dump the powder into it: Drinking it quickly to get it over with, gagging at the taste, he lay back down and sighed as the powder almost immediately began to work. It really was the good stuff. The cheap powders he usually bought took ages to take effect.

A few minutes later, he was fast asleep.

He woke with a start a few hours later to the familiar banging and clanging as buildings shut up for the night, the distant tolling of the temple bells, heralding the closing hour. Rath sat up slowly, sighed happily when nothing hurt quite as badly as it had before. He still felt miserable, but he would be able to grit his teeth and get through the night.

Climbing out of bed, he quickly washed off with cold water and the last bit of soap he had, then pulled on his temple best, since the rest of his clothes were not in a fit state to be showing up to a brothel, even if he'd be taking them right off again.

Downstairs, there was food precisely as promised, though no people. Must have gone to temple or been called away on something else. Rath shrugged and made short work of the day-old bread soaked in broth and stewed vegetables.

He carried the last few bites of bread with him as he headed out, walking as quickly as he could manage across town to Honey Street. Rapping on the back door, he kissed the cheek of the young man who answered, then hurried through the kitchen and down a short hall to Trin's office. "Sorry I'm late!"

"You're not, though barely, by the tolling," she said with a faint smile. "Anyway, I'm not going to complain about a whore who brings in a customer paying double to have you for the night, insisted on waiting for you to arrive, and ordered plenty of food and wine to keep himself occupied. He's in the violet room, move along now. No time for your questions—he's been waiting long enough!"

Rath moved. Who in the names of the Fates would pay that much money for *him*? He was too old to be doing much more whoring, and no one who knew he worked there occasionally ever bothered to demand him especially.

I'll see you tonight.

He stopped dead on the stairs, then resumed walking, stride increasing nearly to a run as he finished the stairs and stormed down the hall to the large room at the end. It was decorated ostentatiously in purple, cream, and gold, and was reserved for the highest-paying clients, usually nobles, but also the occasional merchant.

Throwing the door open, Rath stepped inside and closed it again, then planted his hands on his hips. "What in the buggering Ends are you doing here?"

"You know someone once said those very words at this *very important* dinner I attended? I was twelve. You can imagine how impressed I was by the importance of this *very important* dinner. It was some minor noble, I think, affronted that a man who'd insulted his family had also been invited. I laughed so hard I spit wine out my nose and got it all over my nice, new, snow-white jacket. I thought my mother was going to strangle me with her diamond necklace. Thankfully, she loves those diamonds more than all her children combined, so I was merely banned from *very important* dinners for a couple more years."

Rath rolled his eyes. "You poor thing."

Tress grinned from where he was sprawled lazily across the plush bed, wearing only a dressing robe that he hadn't even bothered to belt closed. "You don't sound very sorry for my awful, awful childhood. The wine was red. I hate red wine."

"Your parents sound quite cruel," Rath replied. "If I have to listen to this all night, *I* shall need some wine, and I'm not picky what color it is."

Laughing, Tress swung his feet over the edge of the bed and stood, walking over to a small table laden with wine and food—even sweets, which Rath never got, save on holy days. He could not fathom what it would be like to be able to eat whatever he wanted, whenever he wanted. He'd probably eat honey cakes every single day and wind up fatter than a pig being led to slaughter.

"What are you doing here?"

"If you have to ask what I'm doing in a brothel, then I have to wonder what exactly they've been making you do."

Rath groaned and sat down, and bugger the *client* if he didn't like Rath's behavior. "I mean what are you doing at this particular brothel? How did you know I'd be here?"

"Oddly enough, there aren't a lot of whores named Rath. It only took asking in a couple of places to figure out where you worked." He smiled like a small child who'd managed to put his clothes on all by himself.

"Spoiled brat." Rath stared, unable not to, as Tress walked over to him. The robe, as purple as the rest of the room and heavily embroidered in gold and silver, looked made to compliment his dark skin. The way it hung open left nothing to the imagination—not that Rath needed imagination. His memory worked just fine.

He stared at the cup Tress held out. "What's that?"

"Wine, idiot. What did you think I was doing?"

Rath shook his head, not certain what to say. He hadn't really paid attention. If a client was feeling generous, they might allow Rath to have any wine or food that was left over. A couple had poured the wine *on* him: one to lap it from his skin and the other in a fit of temper. Nobody poured him wine and brought it to him.

Not certain what else to do, he took a sip. Drew back and stared. Took another, larger sip. "This is amazing."

"It is remarkably good stuff," Tress agreed, wandering away to pour a cup for himself. "I've used this house before, because Mistress Trinira doesn't skimp on anything. Charges heavily for it, but I've never regretted a shilling."

Oh, to know what it was like to count by shillings. Rath drank more wine, because he would be damned if he lost the chance to enjoy something he'd likely never get to have again. He couldn't even be put out that Tress had bought him medicine only to ensure he'd be well enough for tonight. If the man wanted to be eccentric, let him. Rath would enjoy it while it lasted, and Tress would be gone soon enough. "You must want something particularly unusual and extravagant, to be buying me medicine and plying me with your fancy wine."

Tress rolled his eyes as he took a sip from his own cup. "I don't want anything."

"That's a lie."

"Come and get in bed."

So it was a lie. Rath didn't know why that

disappointed him. What had he thought they were going to do? Sit around talking? That would have been unbelievably boring.

He removed his clothes and finished the wine, then strode across the room and obediently climbed into bed. And oofed when a bundle of fabric struck him in the face. He fumbled and finally got a hold of the heavy material, saw it was another dressing robe.

"Much as I enjoy staring at your ass, put that on before you freeze it right off."

Rath frowned, but did as he was told; when it doubt, follow orders. He stood up to pull it on, then climbed back in bed. Tress joined him a moment later, carrying a plate of food and Rath's cup, refilled. He set the food between them, handed off the wine, then pulled something from the pocket of his robe. "I brought you a present." He grinned like a little boy pleased with himself for hiding his mother's cooking spoon.

"I don't want it."

"Oh, now who's being a brat?" Tress replied and dropped the paper-wrapped packet in Rath's lap.

Rath scowled at him but handed off his wine when Tress flicked his fingers, and pulled away the twine and paper. The ornate writing, all loopy and long, took him a little while to puzzle out. He wasn't very amused when he did. *Beginning Manners and Etiquette for Young Persons of Quality.*

"Ha fucking ha," he said, and without even thinking about it, knocked Tress on the head.

He realized his stupidity in the next moment and recoiled, opening his mouth to form an apology—but Tress only laughed and looked even more pleased with himself than he had already. "I knew you'd love it."

"I hate it."

Tress just continued to look pleased with himself. "Well, you could always sell it. Might get a couple of pennies for it. But I'd hold on to it if I were you. It's bad luck to part with a love token."

"Love token? So far you've given me a farthing charm and a book of manners I don't need. No wonder you idiots need a tournament to get married."

Tress laughed hard enough a bit of wine splashed on his hand. "I wish I could deny that, but I would be struck down by the Fates for telling so great a lie. Drink your wine, eat something. I've brought another book. This one is a collection of tales from past tournaments. Thought I could read to you. Maybe you'll learn something useful."

That sounded nicer than Rath would *ever* admit. The whole night was too baffling for him to know what to do with it. "You are the strangest person I have ever met."

"Yes, well, I'm also a paying customer, so do as you're told."

Rath rolled his eyes, used his cup to give a mocking salute. "Yes, Highness."

Tress choked on his wine, then cast Rath a glare. "Stuff it. Lay back and behave, or I'll read the book of manners, and we'll both sleep so hard we won't wake for three days."

"As the customer demands," Rath replied and obeyed because strange as the situation was, he wasn't about to complain enough that Tress changed his mind. It was his money. If he wanted to be eccentric with it, fine. Rath was more than happy to enjoy the food, wine, and Tress's voice as he began to read.

DUEL

Rath sat on one of the many benches that had been set out around the perimeter of twenty different dueling circles. The whole thing was a farce—one thousand people, nearly all of them young idiots who believed this would lead to something more than pain, humiliation, and wasted time. Fighting each other in the saddest excuses for 'dueling' that Rath had ever seen.

It was like somebody had dragged the pit fighting and boxing matches to the fairgrounds instead of keeping them to the empty warehouse of the week at the dockyards.

He gingerly tested his nose, which was sore and a bit swollen, but thankfully not broken. The little brat claiming to be from the west end, but who definitely sounded like he was a little country mouse still learning how not to get his pockets picked, had nearly got him, but Rath was older and bigger, and those two things usually sent cocky striplings fleeing like startled birds.

He'd won two matches so far, but he had to win two more if he stood any chance of being one of the remaining five hundred.

One thousand people had moved forward from the melee. In the dueling round, they had to fight five rounds each, and at the end, the officials tallied all the wins and losses and the top five hundred moved on.

The crier assigned to his ring called his name again. Rath groaned, and next to him, Kelni laughed. She thumped him on the back, urged him to stand. "Fates

See your victory."

"Fates See me sleeping in my bed tonight, alive and well," Rath muttered.

Memories stirred of where he'd slept last night, lulled by Tress's warm, smooth voice as he read Rath stories. Such a frivolous night, and probably the best Rath had ever enjoyed. He'd been more disappointed than he would ever admit aloud that Tress had been gone when he'd woken. There'd been a mark on the pillow instead, but the sight of money had not cheered him the way it normally did.

Hopefully, Tress was starting to become bored. Between Tress and the tournament, Rath had had enough upheaval. He wanted his ordinary life back, before foolish ideas set in and long-dead dreams began to stir.

Given Tress was one of the marriage candidates in the tournament, Rath should be suspicious of his motives for spending so much time and money on a competitor. Then again, what did it matter? Once he had the ten slick, he would have all he needed to pay Friar, and then it was back to his ordinary pattern of work, drink, sleep, and the occasional visit to his mother.

He stepped into the ring as the guard supervising the match gave the signal and faced his opponent: another stripling who must have been at least twenty, but looked closer to fifteen. Rath nearly rolled his eyes as he watched his opponent prepare to charge him while trying not to look like that was exactly what he was doing. Like a hundred other idiots hadn't tried to take him down with an all-out run. Rath was big. That did not mean stupid, as so many people seemed to think. He flexed his fingers and rolled his shoulders, resting lightly on the balls of his feet in preparation for the attack.

The guard dropped his arm and cried, "Begin!" and the youth, predictably, snarled something crude and charged him—

And threw something in Rath's face.

Rath screamed as the powder stung his eyes and face. *That* was low. "Fire powder!" he bellowed, stepping out of the ring, waving one arm in the air and fumbling for his dirty kerchief with the other, since it was all he had. "Fire powder!"

The guard at his ring called a halt and then Rath heard the familiar hard, cracking smack of a gauntleted hand striking bare skin. The idiot would be lucky he didn't wind up with something in his face broken, but Rath didn't much care.

"Here now," said a gentle voice, and someone tugged away the kerchief with which Rath had been futilely trying to wipe away the powder. It was replaced by a damp cloth that smelled of milk and pungent herbs. After a few minutes, the same voice said, "There, try to open them now."

Rath did, though he could only partially manage it. He squinted at the person helping him, a handsome individual wearing the same uniform as the guards, but with yellow sleeves and hood that indicated he was a healer. "Thank you."

"They're still mighty red, be sore for a couple of days, but you probably know that. You seem acquainted, as quickly as you reacted."

"Like a baby!" snarled the idiot who'd thrown the powder. "It wasn't even that much. You just quit like a dishonorable—" He broke off as the guards holding him gave a sound shake.

Rath laughed. "You cheated, but I'm dishonorable for declaring it? You're going to need more sense than that if you plan to keep cheating in fights, stripling."

"I'm not a stripling! Better I win than some old, ugly

sack-slinger—" He yowled as one of the guards clapped his ears.

A guard with Captain's marks gestured sharply. "Get him out of here." He turned to the crier, jerking a thumb at Rath. "Did you mark the win?"

"Yes, sir."

"Then finish up here and move on to the next bout. I want these concluded sometime this century."

"Yes, Captain," the crier said, but the captain had strode off, already yelling at somebody else.

Clearing his throat, the crier turned to Rath. "That's three victories in a row for you."

"I'm not sure it's much of a victory if I won because the other man cheated."

The crier shrugged. "Rules are rules. Cheating is an immediate forfeit. Take your place on the bench, and I'll call you for your next fight, unless you'd like additional rest time due to injury."

Rath shook his head. "I'd rather get this over with."

"As you wish," the crier said, the barest smile curving his perpetually-stern mouth.

Rath sat down and sighed—and looked up as a guard uniform came into view. He looked up at the healer, who handed him a small tin. "What…"

Pressing the tin into his hands, the healer said, "Use this around your eyes to help with the redness and swelling. Not too much, and it will tingle a bit, but it should help speed the healing process."

"I can't accept—"

"Oh, that's enough. Stop arguing with a healer and do as you're told." The healer winked, then strode off before Rath could say anything more. He sighed again, but twisted open the tin, cautiously lifting it to his nose, braced for unpleasantness. But it smelled faintly sweet, and looked something between fresh cream and soft butter. He gingerly dabbed a fingertip in it and rubbed some of it carefully around his sore eyes.

As promised, the ointment tingled, but his eyes did not hurt anywhere near as much. The last time some knave had thrown fire powder in his face, Rath had been stuck washing them with the cleanest water he could find every bell. It had taken just over a week for his eyes to completely recover. Thankfully, it was not long after that the new bailiff took over the city guard and the bastard who'd run it before and all his nasty little knaves had been given a firm booting out of the city.

"What happened to you?" Kelni asked as she dropped down beside him.

"Fire powder."

She stared at him blankly.

Rath snorted. "What do they do for fun in your fishing village? Fire powder—it's a mix of a few cheap herbs that burn everything they touch. Fun in food, not so fun in your eyes. I think it began as something the military used, at least that's what someone told me once, but trust ale stories to your peril." He shrugged. "It's mostly used now by thieves and such, to stall guards and buy extra time. But people will try anything when they're desperate to win."

"I see," Kelni said. "If I want to tell a person to piss off, I throw bad ale or the pisspot in their face. None of this fancy powder you city folk use."

"Fancy? No. It's cheap and rough, and a few pinches here and there never go missing. If I meet that little stripling on the street—" He broke off as his name was called again, cringing inwardly that they kept using his full name. What would it take to make them stop that? "I'll be back. How'd your latest go, by the way?'

Kelni smiled. "Three out of five."

"Good." He strode off with a parting wave and stepped up to his ring. Smiled in pleased surprise when he saw Warloff. One of the few men that made Rath look like a stripling. If he was well known for hauling sacks like they were stuffed with feathers, Warloff was known for moving entire barrels of ale like they were empty and *made* of feathers.

He was also a widower of two years with three young children. Even if Rath had stood a chance of winning this fight, he wouldn't have wanted to. If anyone deserved a safe, warm home and regular meals, it was Warloff and his trio of charming imps. "Ho, Warf."

"Ho, Rat," Warf said cheerfully. "When was the last time we did this? The Stuffed Pig?"

Rath laughed. "I still have the scar on my ribs to show it."

Warf lightly touched his nose, still faintly crooked from the breaking Rath had given it. That had been back when they'd been twenty or so, Rath mostly still whoring, but working the docks from time to time, because the customers liked his muscles and extra pennies were always a good thing. They'd started out not friends, then somehow, one drunken brawl and a half-shilling in damage with another three pennies in fines and bribes… Well, the oddest things turned a man into a friend.

The guard raised his arm and gave the starting cry as he dropped it.

The fight didn't last long, and Rath laughed when the guard called the end. Warf helped him to his feet. "They said you had joined, but I didn't believe it. You're probably the most level-headed of us."

Rath shrugged. "I'm doing what's necessary. How many fights is that for you?"

"Five," Warf said with a grin.

"Fate-favored bastard. You can buy me a pint sometime, and several after you're a lord." Rath clapped him on the arms, and they went their separate ways.

He dropped down on his bench once more, wishing absently for a pint right then. Anything, really. All this dueling was exhausting work. Couldn't they offer up a few sips of something? Bah.

A good portion of the crowd that had been gathered that morning had dispersed, all those who'd definitely been eliminated heading home. Those who remained still totaled more people than would actually pass to the next round.

If he didn't win his last fight, he definitely wouldn't.

His last fight came a few minutes later: another cocky, overexcited youth. She was smarter and trickier than the others, but he'd seen all her moves a hundred times from people much better at them.

She stormed off, red-faced and howling, toward a cluster of friends—one of whom was the boy Rath had first defeated. Well, hopefully he wouldn't be going up against them again any time soon. If he recalled correctly, and if what he remembered of the stories Tress had read was right, the next challenge up would be some manner of hunt or puzzle. It was the only challenge where nobody was disqualified, since its sole purpose was to sort them according to what nobles they'd be competing for.

He sat down on the bench, brightened when a man came over bearing a tray weighed down by cups of not-bad ale, though it was a touch sweeter than Rath usually liked. But free drink was free drink, and he always liked that.

A little while later, they brought around food as well, and he'd just worked up the nerve to help himself to a second round of bread and cheese when the criers called for attention. Rath assembled with his little group and waited to hear his name.

When it came several minutes later, he nearly sank to the ground in relief. Finally, *finally* it was over. He could give Friar his damned money and get back to work. Rent was due soon, damn it, and he really needed to do laundry and see about new boots for the winter season that loomed. Hopefully, his jacket and winter cloak would hold up another year, because he definitely could not afford new ones.

Eventually the reading of the names concluded, and Rath did the already familiar shuffle over to the tables.

He was three people away in line when some of the chatter broke through his thoughts enough for him to overhear one of the clerks admonishing a person in the next line as she collected her ten slick. "—attempt to take the money and not return to compete, you or your relatives will be located and made to repay the debt."

Rath's stomach dropped to his boots. He was an *idiot.* Of course they'd have something in mind to prevent outright theft. He'd been so focused on getting the money and paying off Friar that he hadn't thought what the tournament officials would do if he took their ten slick and ran. Why should they care? But of course they would care—ten slick was a fortune, especially multiplied by five hundred. He was going to have to stick with the tournament until he lost.

His ruined mood did not improve at the reassurance that he would probably lose in the next round. It was only because he'd spent an ill-advised amount of time as a boy getting into scrapes and later as a young man getting into fights that he'd made it this far. His only other skills were hauling sacks and spreading his legs. Whatever puzzle or hunt they'd devised for the sorting round… He wouldn't lose, because it was just sorting. The 'worst' outcome was being sorted into the group that would compete for the chance to marry one of the fifty-four barons. The 'best', of course, was making it into the small group that would compete to marry into the royal family.

Damn it. He was going to have get through the sorting, then lose in the challenge after that. And the sorting could take days, depending on the challenge. Fates knew how long the first challenge of the third round would take. Fates-buggering *fuck*.

When he finally reached the table, Rath almost said bugger it all, but carelessly getting himself dead and dumped in the harbor wasn't going to solve anything. He took his money, listened to the admonition and details about when to show up at the fairgrounds on the morrow, then at last was allowed to head home.

He glanced toward the far end of the field, where people were erecting the stands the nobles would use to watch as the challenges were issued and victories declared, now that the far less interesting preliminaries were nearly finished.

Damn it, he'd wanted to be gone before all that nonsense started up. Heaving a sigh, he increased his pace. The sooner he got back to the city, the sooner he could pay Friar and go drown his frustrations in a pint.

He was halfway there when he realized he kept looking around for Tress. Scowling, he kept his eyes ahead of him. Tress probably had much better things to do than spoil him for another evening. It wasn't like Rath could do anything tonight, anyway, unless Tress wanted to settle for a quick and dirty suck-off in a grimy alleyway.

Hastening through the gates, he hurried across the city to his room, where he fetched the additional five slick he needed. The rest of his money, little though it was, he left in his room, because he'd learned the hard way that Friar was always happy to collect interest.

Back on the streets, he cut across several streets and alleyways until he reached the section of Low City known as East End. It was mostly full of housewares, shops, and craftsman. He and his mother had spent a few months there working for a barrel maker and sleeping in his kitchen at night.

It also boasted an old temple that was too decrepit to be used, but was too expensive to tear down. Thirty-odd years ago, a young man had moved his little gang of thugs and thieves into it, and as his gang and power grew, everyone had taken to calling him Friar. Whatever his name really was, no one who knew it was saying. Knowing Friar, they were all dead or had abruptly decided to find work as sailors.

Two huge figures guarded the main door, such as it was, to the temple. Rath saluted. "Ho, Jen, Pippin. How are my favorite gargoyles?"

Pippin rolled his eyes and grunted. Jen gave one of her toothy, silvery smiles. Rumor had it she'd been a merchant's daughter once, and that was how she'd afforded such fancy tooth repairs. Rath was fairly certain she had always been a street rat as much as the rest of them; she was just exceptional at beating coins out of people. And everyone knew she was one of Friar's favorites. "Get inside," she said. "His patience is about to run out."

"What patience?" Rath muttered as he stepped past them into the damp, moldy, and smoky-smelling temple. The smooth floor had long ago been shattered, most of it cracked, broken, and covered by pools of filthy water.

But beyond the main room, into the private rooms reserved for priests, everything had been repaired and better tended, at least moderately. It smelled heavily of Friar's cologne and the cigarettes his lot were always smoking: the fancy, expensive kind that Rath would never be able to afford.

Another guard, dressed in mismatched armor

probably stolen from at least six places, leered as he saw Rath. "Hello, pretty boy."

Rath snorted. "If you think calling me pretty is going to get you anything, it's no wonder you can't afford more than a farthing whore every second full moon."

The guard's leer turned into a scowl, and his pasty skin turned a splotchy red. "You fucking—"

"Enough!" Friar barked, his head poking out a door. "If you can't resist the taunts of a Fates-damned whore, why am I trusting you to guard anything? Shut your damned mouth and do your job. Rat, get your ass in here and give me my damned money."

Rath stepped by the guard, whose glare promised their conversation wasn't over. "That one isn't going to last long," he said as he stepped into the opulent, over-perfumed room that was Friar's office.

Friar took a seat at a large, heavy wooden desk, the kind Rath had once seen in the office of a merchant who'd called him in as a boy to ask him questions about a theft. It was bigger than Rath's bed, dark and carved all over the front and sides with ornate depictions of animals. The chair Friar sat at was just as absurd. Behind him, on either side of the chair, were more stone-faced guards. Another stood inside the door, and a last one at the window that overlooked a weedy, half-flooded scrap of land that had once been a free garden. "I don't need you telling me that. Only thing I want from you is my fifteen slick."

Pulling out his coin purse, Rath tipped out the fifteen marks into his hand, stomach twisting. His fucking *father*. How much damned money would Rath and his mother have if his useless, Fates-rejected father hadn't forced all of them to bleed their lives away paying his debts so they could live to do it another day? Fifteen slick. That was enough money to take care of him and his mother for a long time.

He balled his hand around the money, then strode up to the desk and slapped the pile of coins on it. "Fifteen slick, on time. Are we even?"

Friar reached out idly, moving slowly, lazily, as he counted out each coin and dropped it into the fat purse sitting at his elbow. Finally, when the last coin had vanished, he leaned back in his chair and drawled, "Even—for now."

"I'm not concerned with debts that don't exist yet. See you around, Friar." He turned around and headed for the door.

"I hear you're in the tournament," Friar called after him.

Rath heaved a sigh. Why in the Fates did Friar care about that? "Where else was I going to get the slick? What's it to you?"

"I like you, Rat, even if I don't always like the way your mouth flaps. There are certain parties extremely interested in winning very particular parts of the tournament. You'd do well to keep your goals modest and be better off getting out of it entirely."

"What?" Rath turned back around. "I signed up to get the money my father owed. I just have to stay in it long enough to lose. Why on earth would I want to marry some hoity-toity who's going to lock me away and pretend I don't exist? And anyway, everyone knows they're rigged."

"Yes, rigged meticulously and expensively over a lot of years. People who work that hard to get what they want don't take kindly to interference," Friar said.

"I'm not interfering with anything," Rath replied with a groan. "I just wanted to pay you off. Anyone who sees me as a threat is a fool."

Friar regarded him pensively, then sighed and said, "Do yourself a favor, Rat, and lose quickly."

"That was the plan all along," Rath said. "But thanks, eminence. It's always so reassuring when you pretend to give a damn about anyone other than yourself."

Friar sighed again. "There's that mouth I hate."

Rath smiled at him, sharp and goading. He knew exactly how much Friar hated his mouth. Friar mostly favored women, but only mostly, and Rath had earned quite a few pennies at Trin's place servicing Friar. "Goodnight, Friar."

"Until next we meet," Friar replied, smile just as full of teeth and taunt.

Out in the hall, the temperamental guard had been replaced by a much calmer one that Rath knew well. "G'night, Bones."

"G'night, Rat. Have a care where you crawl."

Rath lifted a hand in lazy farewell and hit the streets again, biting back an urge to laugh. The first few times he'd done this, he *had* laughed, mostly so he wouldn't cry. But everything grew tedious with time, and paying Friar had worn out long ago.

Friar's warning to stay out of the tournament tried to pick at him, but Rath ignored it. He was going to lose the moment he reached the first challenge of the final round. Whatever games other people were playing, they had nothing to do with him.

Hauling back to his part of the city, he quickly retrieved his coin from his room then headed to the Mellow Harp, which had been the favored pub for him and his friends for years, right around the time he'd quit whoring full-time. The place was already busy when he got there, and it took only a glance to locate his friends. They waved at him, and Rath signaled he'd be there in a moment.

Going up the bar, he ordered an ale and bowl of fish chowder. When he got it, he carried the lot over to the table and took the open space on the bench between Coor and Toph. "How'd the fighting go, Coor? I saw you made it as far as me."

"Yeah, but I only won three rounds." Coor shrugged, grinned. "You're the only one left of this ugly lot. If you become a Duke's spouse, you'd better come down here and buy us the whole damned pub."

"Ha," Rath said. "Don't put any money on it. I'm sure you'll all be buying me conciliatory ales in a few more days."

"Well, you're still the winner for now so buy *me* an ale," Coor said with a grin.

Rath heaved a long, aggrieved sigh, but when a server came round, he gave her two pennies to keep the ale coming.

He'd just about finished his third ale when the table went quiet and half of them stared, then broke into smirks and goading grins. "Your suitor is back, Rath."

"I don't have a suitor," Rath said irritably. "What are you blathering—?" he broke off as realization knocked him upside the head, and he twisted in his seat to see that, sure enough, Tress was walking toward them, that idiotic smile on his face. "What in the buggering Fates is he doing here?"

The others laughed, and Toph elbowed him in the ribs. "You're certainly the busy one these days. Winning the tournament and snaring a handsome lord to keep on the side."

"I'm not winning or snaring anything," Rath snapped. "But I will shove your head into the table if you don't stuff it."

Toph rolled his eyes. "Somebody has a raw dick."

"Your snatch is about to—" he broke off as a hand fell heavy on his shoulder and scowled up at Tress's stupidly handsome face. "Hello, again."

Tress's smile widened. "I'm sorry I missed you after

70

your duel. When my father decides to talk, he'll try to go until the seas run dry, and if I dare to leave while he's still going, I usually wind up *in* the sea. But I don't want to interrupt you and your friends..." Rath's friends, helpful bastards that they were, immediately assured Tress he was welcome to do with Rath as he pleased so long as he bought them more ale first. Tress laughed and dropped several pennies on the table. "Will that cover it?"

Their cheers of approval were enough to draw the attention of the rest of the noisy pub. Rath finished his own ale, then rose and stormed out. He hadn't made it far down the street when he heard someone coming up behind him, felt the already familiar feel of Tress's fingers wrapping around his arm. "Rath—"

Rath sighed and turned away, gently tugging free of Tress's hold. "What?"

"Did I do something wrong? I thought—" He broke off with a frown, eyes skittering way. "I thought you'd be happy to see me."

Lords were far too complicated for something as simple as *happy.* "It's one thing to approach me, but I don't need you interrupting me and my friends and throwing coin around like a few pennies are nothing to you."

"I'm sorry," Tress said. "I was trying to play along. I didn't mean to overstep."

Rath made a frustrated noise. "Forget it. What do you want?"

Tress's brows rose. "To spend time with you, of course. Isn't that obvious?"

"We aren't friends," Rath said. "We had fun, and you were more than kind to me last night, but we both know this will end in a few days or weeks when you get bored and move to someone or something else."

Mouth flattening, Tress replied, "That's an awful lot

to assume after just a few encounters. You know nothing about me or my motives."

"You're right. I know nothing about you, but you know where I live, where I drink, where to find me whenever it strikes your fancy to do so. I'm completely at your mercy, *my lord.* That will never change throughout all the time we spend together. And frankly, I don't want to keep wasting my limited free time on a man who's eventually going to toss me aside and forget all about me."

"You could give me a fair chance," Tress snapped.

Rath scoffed. "Ask anyone here how often lords prove worthy of a fair chance. High City are all the same, coming down here to slum it and fuck a few grateful commoners, throw some pennies around, and then go back to your High City lives without a care for the hurts and aggravations you've caused down here."

"You're the knave fighting in a tournament to become High City," Tress snapped.

"I'm in the tournament to pay my father's debts so I don't wind up floating in the harbor," Rath replied with a snarl. "I'd quit now if they weren't going to demand I return the money I no longer have. I'd rather have my damned throat slit than become one of you lot."

"Fine," Tress said, voice trembling briefly before he visibly tamped down on his anger and his expression smoothed out. "I guess all Low City are the same, too. Incapable of caring about anything but money, but the whores are good at pretending otherwise if you pay them enough."

Rath recoiled, flinching as though struck. Before he could recover, Tress had stormed off and vanished around the corner. Rath swallowed, feeling raw and cut open. He'd wanted…

Fates, he didn't know what he'd wanted.

No. That wasn't true. He'd wanted it over with

before he did something stupid like get attached.

At least Tress's nasty parting shot confirmed everything Rath had said. If their fight hadn't happened tonight, it would have happened later, and been all the uglier and more painful for the delay. He'd done the right thing getting rid of Tress now.

But he still felt sick to his stomach and ready to put his fist through a window. Laughter spilled out of the pub as the door opened briefly, and it was like salt in his wounds. Shoulders hunched, Rath turned away and headed home, grateful when he was finally able to fall into his creaky little bed and ignore the world for a few precious hours.

He'd get some sleep, and everything would be better in the morning.

SORTING

Three days later, Rath felt worse than he ever had about anything. He anxiously swept his gaze over the crowds as he headed out of the city and down to the fairgrounds, but no matter how hard he looked, he still saw no sign of Tress. But it had always been Tress who had found him, and if he were in Tress's position, he'd be making damn certain Rath didn't see him.

And as he'd stupidly pointed out the night of their fight, he knew nothing about Tress that would let him find the man somewhere else. His only hope was that since Tress had admitted he was one of the marriage candidates, Rath would eventually see him somewhere on the fairgrounds.

Strictly speaking, the candidates and their families were not allowed to interact with the competitors, since it could indicate favoritism, cheating... If they got caught together, Tress would be in a world of trouble, and Rath would be disqualified. Which meant he'd have to pay back the ten slick.

So it was definitely for the best that he'd driven Tress away.

Rath still felt wretched and sick at heart about it, even three days later. He shouldn't, but should never had much to do with anything.

When he reached the blue tent he was thoroughly sick of, he slumped to the ground and wished the whole stupid day was already over. Hopefully today, he would finally get to do the maze. The first day they'd drawn lots, and Rath's number had been all the way at the bottom. Technically, the whole thing was supposed to run five days, but the criers had said to show up two days early because things tended to move quickly, since as one person finished the maze, another was sent straight in.

"You've been looking rather glum for a person who's made it this far," Kelni's familiar, friendly voice greeted.

Rath pushed to his feet and mustered a smile. "Tired, sore, would rather be abed, you know?"

"Mmm," Kelni said. "I do miss home, but I'd rather win a new home that'll see me and mine never live on fish heads and stale bread six months of every year, while the nobles throw out more fish than they eat."

"Very true," Rath murmured.

He was grateful the horns rang before the conversation could continue. He didn't want to talk to anyone but Tress. The only good thing about the past two days was that he'd found time to work, get his laundry done, and buy some staples to keep in his room.

"Competitors!" The crier announced from his barrel. He clapped his hands until everyone had quieted. Once they'd done so, he rattled off the ten starting numbers. Only twenty or so away from Rath's number. He'd be waiting a few hours, but that was better than waiting the whole day. He might actually be able to buy some food and ale and just relax in his room for the night.

The first ten shuffled off toward the enormous maze that had been constructed in the large field beside the fairgrounds. Time was marked for each person as they entered the maze, again when they reached the center, and at the end when they came out of the maze.

When everyone was finished, their times would be combined with their melee and duel scores, and the top ten would be competing for 'the honor of marrying His Royal Highness Prince Isambard'. The next fifty would compete for the six duchies, the next hundred for the seventeen earldoms, and the remaining for the fifty-four baronies.

At least it was a maze. Even Rath's foul mood cheered slightly at the thought. He'd always loved the little mazes they set up for children during the Spring Festival and the Harvest Festival. They were one of his fondest memories, some of the only days where he was allowed simply to play. There hadn't been much chance for leisure growing up, but even his Counter-Fate mother had always taken him to the city celebrations on festival days. He'd do the mazes over and over until he got hungry or someone made him stop. Had always felt a pang walking by them on his way to or from work once he'd gotten too old for such things.

He found a bare strip of grass and stretched out, wrapping his threadbare cloak about him to ward off the worst of the chilly morning. A couple more weeks and there'd be frost. The tournament was not going to be fun going then, but there was too much work to be done to do it any other time of the year.

If he was a fancy lord whose fate was resting on the tournament, a lord who generally preferred to have his nose buried in a book, where would he be? Rath sighed. He'd be safely in his comfortable home reading a damned book and forgetting completely about the ungrateful whore who'd told him to go away.

Rath was such a fucking fool.

He dozed for a bit, stirring whenever the horns announced another competitor had completed the challenge. He was about to go mad with waiting when they finally called his name. Practically leaping to his feet, he hastened over to the crier, who motioned to one of the two north-facing entrances.

The clerk stationed there consulted a fancy little watch that was slowly becoming popular amongst High City folk. He marked something by Rath's name, then looked at him. "You are not allowed to mark the paths, walls, or anything else within the maze. You are not allowed to speak to any other competitor you may encounter. When you reach the center, you will be given a flag by the officials there. I will give you a slip of paper that they will request. They'll return it with the flag, and when you come out of the maze again, give both to me or another clerk. Once we've marked you, take both to the high table. If you do not emerge after two hours, you automatically fail the challenge and default to competing for the baronies. Any questions?" Rath shook his head. The clerk jotted something on a small scrap of paper and handed it to Rath. Once he'd taken it and tucked it away, the clerk said, "Begin."

Rath headed into the maze, heart pounding, mind scrabbling frantically. He shouldn't *care*, but now that he was doing it, the desire to do well sprang to the fore.

He went left at the first split, heart pounding harder when it didn't immediately lead to a dead end. The second split he went right and that *did* dead end. He backtracked carefully, kept going, marking every twist and turn on his arm with his nail the way he'd done as a youth while still trying to learn the city and the docks without getting hopelessly lost.

How long it took him to find the center, he had no way of knowing. It felt like at least an hour had passed, but hopefully, the way back would move faster.

There was a cluster of guards and clerks at the very center of the large square. One clerk snapped his fingers. "The slip of paper they gave you at the start."

Rath pulled it from his coin purse and handed it over. The clerk grunted, looked at him with something that almost seemed like approval, and said to one of the guards, "Purple."

"Really?" The guard smiled as he bent to pull a small square of purple cloth from the chest in the center of the cluster. He handed it to Rath, and the clerk handed over the slip of paper again with new markings upon it. Tucking everything away once more, Rath gave them an awkward salute and trekked back, following the marks on his arm to get out of the maze.

Winding up where he started, he promptly dug out the slip of paper and purple flag and handed them over. Like the other clerk, this one gave him a startled look. He gestured to the nearby guards. "Gold."

"Gold it is," the guard said with an easy grin and pulled a bit of dark yellow cloth from the sack at his hip. "There you go."

"Thank you," Rath said. The clerk handed back his slip of paper and purple flag, and Rath carried it all over to the tables.

The clerk there perked up the same as the other two. Had he done well? Done poorly? He wasn't sure which he preferred, but it didn't matter since he had every intention of doing whatever it took to lose the first challenge of the final round.

"Well done, competitor," the clerk said formally but with a smile. "What's your name?"

"Rathatayen."

Her expression turned sympathetic. She glanced at the slip of paper, nodded to herself, then shuffled through the papers in front of her and made several marks by his name. Half the names on that page had been completely marked out. Had they not shown or something?

Looking up again, the clerk said, "Report here tomorrow at the market bell, just in case everything finishes early. If it looks like the challenge will continue throughout the day, they'll send you away, and you should come again the same time the day after. If you are not here when the sorting announcement is made, you will be disqualified. The challenges will begin on lenday and will take up all of your time for the next three months. Make certain that you tell anyone who needs to know. You will be given suitable time for rest, food, and so forth. Should you ever fail to complete a challenge, you will be immediately disqualified. Further rules will be explained after the sorting ceremony. Any questions?"

"No," Rath said.

"Give me your left hand, then," the woman said. Rath frowned but offered his hand. She wrapped a bit of string around his second finger, then made more notes by his name. "All right, you are free to go for the day."

"Thank you." Slipping away, Rath slowly made his way back to the city, once more looking anxiously around for any sign of Tress. But even in and around the spectator seats, Rath could not spot him. Well, what had he expected? For Tress to seek him out after everything Rath had said? Rath was more likely to win the tournament.

Not that he had forgotten what Tress had said, either. It *was* completely like a noble to sling around those kinds of insults the very moment they didn't get what they wanted. He hadn't realized how much he'd wanted Tress to be different until he'd proven to be just like all the rest.

Rath still kept hoping they'd both been wrong and might make amends, even if they once more went their separate ways in the end.

He tried to shove the fretting over Tress aside as he reached the gates. He had plenty of other matters to worry about and also happier things to focus on. Like going to see his mother to tell her all was well for the present. He might even have penny enough to buy her a sweet.

Yes, that was what he'd do. Buy his mother a sweet and tell her the good news. It was too late in the day to pick up work, anyway, and Trin wasn't expecting him, so he could enjoy a few hours with his mother and then have the whole rest of the night to himself.

Heading quickly across town, he waved to Anta as he slipped in the back door and quickly climbed the stairs to his room. He washed his face and hands, combed his hair, then retrieved his money from its hiding place in the wall behind his bed.

All set, he hit the streets again and headed out on the long walk up Low City, bound for the common bridge. He'd almost reached the end of Apple Street when men grabbed him up and shoved him into a narrow alleyway—too narrow for him to slip by the three men blocking him into it.

Rath swore loudly. Had his father pissed off Friar again already? But no, he knew most of Friar's goons, and at least one familiar face would have come along— if only for the personal pleasure of getting back at Rath for some comment he probably shouldn't have made.

These guys were unfamiliar and wore the kinds of clothes that wealthy people, or the goons that worked for wealthy people, wore when they were trying to blend into Low City. Tress dressed similarly, but on him it had somehow been charming.

On these men it was ominous because it meant he'd pissed off someone with money, which in Low City usually meant he was going to wind up floating in the harbor.

The man in the center of the cluster sneered. "Been looking for you, you uppity little whore."

"Piss off," Rath said. "I haven't been bothering anyone."

"You're bothering plenty," the man in the center said, baring his teeth in a smile probably meant to be threatening. It lacked something due to the missing and broken teeth. He surged forward and grabbed Rath by the front of his shirt, twisted, and slammed him into the wall. Pain burst in the back of Rath's skull and his thigh, where it struck a broken, sharp-edged bit. He could feel blood, hot and sticky, soaking into his pants and running down his leg. "If you know what's good for you, you'll not show up to the tournament tomorrow, understand?"

"If I don't show up, they'll want back the marks they gave me!" Rath said. "I don't need the city guard coming after me anymore than I need you."

The man thumped him against the wall again, then dropped him to the ground and kicked him in the stomach. "Guess you'd better get out of it quickly, then. You ain't gone after the first challenge, you'll find yourself regretting it sorely, understand?"

Rath would have happily replied that he did, but he was too busy not being able to breathe. The man gave a mean laugh, kicked him again, then bent and rifled roughly through his clothes. Rath tried to push him away, but the man just swatted his hand off, slammed his face into the ground so hard that Rath's nose started bleeding, and finally found the coins stashed in an inner pocket of Rath's jacket. He fumbled around a bit more, then after a painful warning squeeze to Rath's injured thigh, signaled to his men and departed.

Tears stinging his eyes, Rath just concentrated on breathing until it mostly didn't hurt to do that. Then he focused on sitting up, a difficult task between his scraped palms, injured thigh, and two solid kicks to his gut.

Standing was even less fun.

There went his plans to visit his mother. Not

wanting to distress her aside, all his money was gone. Trin wouldn't let him work as banged up as he was. Even working the streets wasn't an option. And he wouldn't be able to work in the morning, because he still had the tournament to endure.

Friar hadn't been wrong about Rath making people mad. But why? He was nobody, a laborer and whore and occasional pickpocket. He'd been planning to fail out of the tournament anyway, exactly like he'd told pretty much anyone who'd asked. There was no reason to go beating him up in the alley.

He sniffled as he limped slowly to the edge of the alleyway, then forced the tears back. They wouldn't lessen the pain, and his face hurt enough from the mistreatment and lingering soreness from the fire powder. Looking carefully around, he crept out of the alleyway then slowly, painfully headed back home.

Preferring to avoid people, he walked around to the back of the house and stepped into the kitchen door, relieved that Anta wasn't there. He made for the stairs as quickly as he could, then climbed them step by agonizing step until he finally reached his room.

All he wanted to do was collapse in bed and stay there, pretend he hadn't just gotten beaten and robbed in an alleyway. Thank the Fates he'd already paid rent.

Lowering himself to the floor, he slowly pulled off his boots and set them aside. Bracing his hands on the wall and gritting his teeth, he pulled himself back to standing and worked on peeling off his bloody breeches and drawers. Both were so stained, and the breeches so badly torn, that there would be no salvaging them. He only had one other set of day clothes, damn it, and only four total pairs of drawers, and one was a nice pair to wear with his temple best.

He threw the ruined clothes in a corner to give to Anta later. She could at least do something with the bits that were salvageable. Stripping off the rest of his clothes and hanging them on their hooks, Rath limped over to the washbasin and cleaned up his bloody face and leg as best he could. Thankfully his nose wasn't broken, and the wound on his thigh should stop bleeding now he wasn't constantly stressing it.

Limping over to the bed, he carefully stretched out on it and pulled up his blankets. That would be more laundry to deal with, but it was too cold to go without blankets. Sniffling into his pillow, he let pain and misery drag him down into sleep.

When he woke, it was to the early morning din of people headed out to find work at the docks or with various merchants, milling about to talk to the lamplighters still snuffing lamps and the night-cleaners heading home. Every part of him hurt, even more than when he'd lain down. He slowly sat up, wincing at the rough fabric rubbing against his injured thigh. Sitting would obviously be a fun endeavor for the next several days. He shouldn't have been so quick to give away those twists of medicine.

A different hurt entirely flared in his chest, settled there like a bruise. Rath stared at the little book and charm lying on the floor next to his bed. He'd barely paid either any mind since he'd put them there, but in the past few days, they'd been a constant reminder of the words he would give anything to take back.

He bent over and picked the objects up, ran his thumb over the already-flaking paint on the cheap little charm. Setting it on his pillow, he traced the fancy lettering on the cover of the book. *Beginning Manners and Etiquette for Young Persons of Quality.* He wasn't certain what baffled him more: that High City folk needed books to learn manners, or that this was a *beginning* book.

Curious and grateful for any distraction from the

pain, Rath flipped the book open, frowning when it stuck and *wouldn't* open. He ran his finger along the pages and swore when it scraped over metal unexpectedly along the side. A catch. The book locked? Why in the Fates…

He caught the tiny catch with the edge of a ragged nail and flipped it up, then finally opened the book—and dropped it in shock, sending pennies rolling and scattering over the floor.

Disregarding pain, Rath went around the room retrieving them, wincing and swearing the whole time. When he was finally done, he resumed sitting on the bed and carefully put all the pennies back in their slots. The book wasn't a book at all, but contained two 'pages' filled with special little slots meant to hold pennies. The slots were too small and shallow to hold any other coin. All told, the book held twenty-four pennies—one short of a shilling.

It was more money than he'd ever had at once that he got to *keep*. And Tress had given it to him… why, exactly? Rath would never know.

Damn it, he'd gotten rid of Tress for good reason. Look how nasty Tress had turned at the end. It just confirmed that Rath had done the right thing. If he'd let it continue, let himself get attached, how much worse would it have been in the end? He'd never wanted to be the plaything of some hoity-toity, anyway.

It didn't matter why Tress had given him the money. Twenty-four pennies was nothing to someone like Tress. Fates, he'd left an entire mark on the pillow after their night together.

A night where he'd done nothing but give Rath food and wine and read him stories. Rath sighed and set the book aside, standing to get dressed as the morning prayer bell began to ring. He only had about an hour to get to the fairground, and he'd just barely make it, given how slowly he was moving.

When he was dressed, he picked out two pennies from the book then tucked it away in his hiding place. Limping out of the room and downstairs, he headed out the back of the shop and around to the street, waving to Anta on his way and pretending not to hear when she called after him.

People thronged the streets, a mixture of the usual morning bustle threaded with bumbling out-of-towners. Rath paused at a vendor near the gate to buy breakfast, savoring the taste of fresh bread sticky with honey.

He tensed when someone bumped into his shoulder, jarring his whole body and making him hiss in pain— but they continued on, and Rath tried to relax. The muggers had delivered their warning, and they'd said to be certain he lost in the first challenge. They probably wouldn't bother him again until after that.

When he finally reached the fairgrounds, he resisted the temptation to sit down. If he did that, he wasn't certain he'd be able to get back up. Given the maze was gone and a stage had been set up in front of the stands, clearly the sorting challenge was over, and they'd be announcing the sorting that day.

Instead, he simply found a bit of empty space where he could see most everyone coming toward him, and tried not to jump every time he heard footsteps close behind him.

The back of his thigh felt hot and sticky, which meant his only other pair of everyday breeches was ruined, but there was nothing he could do about it. At least they were dark enough that the blood was probably going unnoticed.

Why. That was what upset him the most. He was nothing, no one. One of hundreds of competitors who would be competing to marry into one of the fifty-four baronies. At most, if the Fates were feeling particularly perverse, he might have ranked high enough to compete for an earldom. So what? Who cared if he competed to marry the third daughter of earl number fourteen? It wasn't like he would have succeeded in doing so anyway, the way everything was rigged. Even the laziest idiot could pick the false peasants out of the crowd. Just glancing around, Rath could see three of them. Nothing stood out like a wealthy person trying to pretend they'd grown up poor.

Why beat him up over a matter that had been settled years ago?

Whatever, it didn't matter. They weren't telling him to do anything he hadn't been planning to do already. That didn't keep him from stewing over the question incessantly anyway, and acerbating his foul mood.

Nothing had ever sounded sweeter than the trumpets signaling the beginning of the official sorting.

"Competitors!" called a crier, throwing out his arms, voice pitched louder than any Rath had so far heard. He was dressed in blue and purple livery trimmed in gold braiding, marking him as the crier in charge, though Rath didn't know the exact title. He stood in the center of a large stage. "Welcome and challenge well met. Congratulations to you!" He turned to his right and said, "Honored nobles, be most welcome! Your Most Royal Majesty, we are most honored by your presence."

Rath swallowed and turned around. He'd been so lost in thought that he hadn't properly appreciated that the stands were filled with people. And all the way at the top, hidden behind thin, gauzy material to retain some of their privacy and safety, were the king and queen, and possibly the whole royal family.

The nobles were a mass of rich, vibrant colors and the occasional flash of gold and jewels. Now that he was paying attention, Rath could smell snatches of perfume on the air, succulent food piled on tables for them—food he'd never be able to afford even with nearly a whole shilling to his name.

And for the competitors… nothing. If this went on long enough, they might hand out ale, bread, and cheese like they had the other day. How typical of the hoity-toity to feed themselves well but give scraps to those toiling away on their behalf. Rath's lip curled as he turned away.

"Competitors, first we will call the names for those competing for the honor of marrying into the family of our most honorable Earls. As your name is called, please come to the stage to collect your competitor ring and return to your place once you have it."

Rath sighed as they began reading out the names of the one hundred people competing for the earldoms, his mind drifting right back to fretting itself to death, until a horn sounded again, and they moved on to the duchies. At least there were only six of those, though it still took some time to list off the fifty qualifying competitors.

Could he just leave? No, they probably had rings for the three hundred-odd competing for the baronies, so he'd have to remain to collect his once they were done with the others.

When they finally finished the duchies, he was cranky and in pain enough to want to cry, and would it really be all that difficult to pass around ale or tea or *something?*

The crier raised his arms for silence, lowered them slowly a couple of minutes later, and called out, "Now, honored guests and brave competitors, we announce the ten remarkable people who will be competing for the incomparable honor of marrying His Most Royal Highness Prince Isambard."

Rath huffed, shoulders slumping with fatigue and pain. Ten names. He could make it through ten more names and shuffling through a long line to get his stupid ring.

"Terra Cobbler," the crier announced, and a small woman climbed the stage with a happy grin. She was handed a ring, then a guard motioned for her to stand at the far end of the stage. "John Black!" A small smattering of cheers as a large man climbed the stage.

"Helena Copper! Sarie Thatcher!" Two more women climbed the stage. "Jessa Tanner." A tall, thin, handsome man climbed the stage, one of those Rath had picked out earlier as not-actually-poor. The pleased, not even remotely surprised look on his face only confirmed it.

Fates, he just wanted to be done with the whole rotten day. And it had barely begun. Would anyone miss him if he just went back to bed and stayed there until tomorrow?

"Rathatayen Jakobson!"

Rath's breath stopped. What? He stared wide-eyed at the stage, certain he must have misheard.

Then someone—Warf—hissed his name and came rushing over, gave him a gentle shove.

Swallowing, trying to get his lungs to function properly again, Rath walked on trembling legs to the stage. A guard smiled warmly, clapped him on the shoulder, and presented him with a small copper ring. Rath took it, saw his name and a strange mark inscribed on the inside. The outside was decorated with swirling, curling lines—Fate lines, they were called. You couldn't enter a temple without tripping over the pattern.

Rath still couldn't breathe properly as he was shuffled across the stage and took his place next to the smarmy man whose name he'd already forgotten. Rath hadn't done anything. He wasn't supposed to be on stage and headed for the final round of challenges. He certainly shouldn't be on stage as a competitor for the *royal family*. Oh, Fates, he was going to pass out.

The remaining names were called, but Rath didn't hear them. He looked around the crowd in front of the stage, the nobles off to the side. He didn't belong here. This was *stupid*. He'd just wanted to pay off a debt. How in the names of the Holy Fates was he competing for the chance to marry a prince?

And what about the men who'd beaten him yesterday? Had they known? How?

More importantly, would they really let him live long enough to lose the first challenge?

When they finally let him off the stage, Rath hurried away as quickly as he could, ignoring everyone who called after him, pushing his way through the crowd even though doing so hurt. He got as far as a scraggly copse of trees before he lost his breakfast.

Rath sat back in the grass when there was nothing left to heave up, stomach hurting anew from the unpleasant treatment, sweat drying tacky on his skin, entire body throbbing with pain, and his thigh hot from the abuse. He just wanted to be left alone. No beatings. No threats. No scrambling desperately to come up with alarming sums of money. No more whoring. Just work and the pub and the occasional day off to do something fun.

How had his situation gone from bad to worse? He didn't want to marry a damned prince. He didn't want to marry anybody.

Even if he did, there was nobody in the world who wanted to marry *him*. Not with his whoring background. Not with his troublesome father. Not when it was known he was tangled up with Friar. He was a loser, and even a tournament intended to improve the lot of losers was never going to change that.

Drawing his knees up, Rath folded his arms across them and buried his head in his arms, focused on breathing and calming down and not succumbing to the urge to start screaming.

"Rath?"

The voice was a kick in the gut far more brutal than the two he'd received last night. Rath dragged his head up, praying to the Fates he was imagining it.

Hope shattered like an egg dropped on cobblestones as he stared up at Tress's stupid, handsome face.

RECONCILIATION

Tress stared back at him wide-eyed. "What happened to you?"

"Nothing," Rath replied, slowly unfolding and pushing himself to his feet. "Excuse me, my lord." He brushed by Tress, heart pounding even harder than it had when the crier had called his name.

He'd wanted to see Tress again. Why was he running?

Trying to run, anyway. He hadn't made it more than six paces when Tress snagged his arm and drew him to a halt. "Rath, what *happened* to you?"

"Meaning no disrespect, my lord, but I've already answered that question."

Tress's mouth tightened, eyes pulled tight at the edges. "You were lying."

Rath glared. "I'm not obliged to tell you the truth, my lord. In fact, I'm not obliged to tell you anything. And as you so clearly stated, whores are good at lying. Good day to you." He pulled free and did his best to storm off, but the attempt was feeble given his damned leg wouldn't stop bleeding.

Couldn't a man lick his wounds and be terrified and miserable in peace? He just wanted to be left *alone*. Not beaten up. Not dragged up on stage. Not made to run around. Not forced to confront Tress in the middle of the road after he'd already made a fool of himself vomiting like a drunk. His eyes stung, and his head was beginning to throb.

"Rath, *please.* I'm sorry."

The words were another punch to the gut, a surprise so unexpected that the wind was knocked right out of him. Rath stopped. Tress circled around to stand in front of him, lifting a hand and reaching out—and letting it fall away at the last minute. "Your leg is bleeding, and that's obviously not the only reason you're in pain. Let me help, please?" As if he could see or sense Rath wavering, he added, "I'm begging you."

Rath's stomach flip-flopped, and he relented with a sigh. "I just need rest. You can't help with that."

Tress lifted his eyes to the sky and heaved the world's most long-suffering sigh. "You sound just like my brothers. Oh, it's only a small, severely-bleeding sword wound. I can keep practicing! You're all idiots. Come on." He reached out again, lightly touching Rath's hand. When Rath didn't pull away, Tress took his hand and tugged Rath to stand next to him before resuming walking. He opened and closed his mouth a couple of times, scowling at the ground and in the end not saying anything.

Rath gently tugged his hand free, but kept walking alongside him—or tried to, anyway. His leg was hurting more and more. It was a good thing he didn't want to win the first challenge, because he was barely in shape to even show up.

The last time he'd endured a silence this miserable, he and his mother had been thrown out of their current home and his mother had been figuring out how to tell him they were going to have to sleep on the streets again for a little while.

He stumbled, but instead of hitting the ground, he just wound up bundled close against Tress. "I'm guessing you won't let me have a horse or chair summoned so you don't have to walk?"

"I don't know how to ride, and I wouldn't climb

dead into one of those stupid chairs," Rath replied.

Tress sighed. "That's what I thought. Will you at least let me help you? You'll do irreparable damage to that leg if you keep pushing it so hard."

"It'll be fine," Rath replied, but he didn't argue when Tress took most of his weight and helped him limp along, around to the city gate and through it. "Where are we going?"

The barest smile teased at the corners of Tress's mouth. "I'm not telling, because you'll just fuss and bluster more."

Rath huffed, but didn't deny it.

"What happened to you? This didn't happen in the tournament."

"Muggers," Rath said. "I really will be fine in a few days. I've been in worse pub fights." When he was ten years younger.

"So much like my brothers," Tress muttered. "My middle brother is about your age, I think. You two could compete for most stubborn idiot."

Rath barely heard anything after *brother is about your age.* "Your *brother* is my age. What age are *you*?"

Tress's sour face said he very much wished he'd thought harder about his words. "I'm twenty-eight."

"You're five years younger than me." Rath closed his eyes.

"It's not that much of a difference!"

Rath cast him a look. "Saying that with a sulky frown on your face does not help your cause."

"I'm not sulking."

Rath laughed. "If you say so." Tress gave him a cautious smile, and Rath's laughter collapsed as he remembered to add, "My lord."

Tress sighed and looked away. "You're never going to forgive me, are you? I suppose that's fair, but I had hoped…" He shook his head. "We're here." He tried to usher Rath inside before he got a good look at the building, but he seemed to have forgotten that Rath had grown up in Low City. He knew it better than the guards that were supposed to patrol it, and probably better than most of the criminals who took advantage of the lazy guards.

He definitely recognized the home of the West End healer who thought himself too good to deal with 'East End rabble'. He dealt almost exclusively with the merchants, craftsmen, and other 'better' portions of Low City. The only time he treated rabble was during his required three days of service at the temple each month. He wasn't anyone Rath had ever interacted with, but he'd heard plenty of stories from his friends and other people in the bars and at work.

The healer came bustling out of a back room with the chiming of the bell above the door, scowled when he saw Rath, but as he was opening his mouth, he got a longer look at Tress and immediately snapped it shut again. "Hello, I am Healer Grane. How may I help you?" he asked.

Rath snorted, but Tress spoke first. "How do you think, man? My friend here is obviously hurt. Do you know your trade or not?"

"What's wrong, exactly?" Grane asked, motioning for them to cross the room to join him at a large, flat, smooth table. Another table nearby held an assortment of bottles, boxes, twisting papers, herbs, and other healing components and tools.

"My thigh," Rath said, before Tress could. "I was mugged yesterday, and my thigh was slashed by a bit of broken wall."

"Breeches off and on the table, then. Let's get a look at it," Grane replied.

Rath grimaced inwardly, but stripped off his ruined breeches and drawers and climbed up on the table, though it was an awkward, fumbling effort at best, and he needed Tress's help. He buried his flushed face in his folded arms, wishing he were anywhere but there. After four miserable days, this was how he and Tress started talking again? Him injured and his bare ass in the air while a grouchy healer poked and prodded? On the other hand, given the tumult of his life lately, he wasn't certain why he'd thought it would go any other way.

He winced as cool fingers fussed with the wound, followed by a cold substance that stung at first, but then mellowed and warmed and made that whole part of his leg all tingly. It also made him sleepy. Grane was talking, and Rath was just aware enough to notice he'd started slipping a bit of High City into his accent, but then the drowsiness sunk its claws in deep and pulled him down.

A clattering sound jerked him awake, and Rath sat up with a start and mumbled curse. "Where—what—?" He groaned and let his head fall back down. "Where am I?"

"The healer's," replied Tress. "He says you appear to be sensitive to murgot, as quickly as you fell asleep after he applied it to your wound."

Rath groaned again, then tried to sit up. A warm, heavy hand on his back stalled the movement. He tried to focus on that, fight the urge to fall right back to sleep.

"You really did react strongly, and it was just a cream to help with the wound."

"Mushrooms," Rath mumbled. "I always act funny around stupid mushrooms. I ate a blue drop mushroom once as a child and almost died. Hate the damned things."

Tress's fingers curled against his back briefly before relaxing again. "I'm sorry. I should have thought to ask. My sister has a similar reaction to sunrise flowers."

"Don't worry about…" Rath said and drifted off again.

When he woke again, it was to a dimly-lit room he'd definitely never seen before. An expensive room, given the size of the bed, the beeswax candles, the food spread out on a table in the corner, and no fewer than three colorful, woven rugs on the floor. Fates be merciful, where was he?

A soft hitch of breath made him jump, and he turned to the source, only then realizing he wasn't alone in the enormous bed. Tress was fast asleep behind him, lying on top of the blankets, shoes gone, but still in his stockings, a book splayed open on his chest.

Rath swallowed, heart giving a lurch. Tress had said he was sorry. Had taken Rath to a healer. The way his head felt heavy, cloudy, the healer must have given him something with murgot. He vaguely remembered… not much. Talking. Tress apologizing again, maybe. He groaned and rubbed his temples. Stupid mushrooms.

His stomach growled as the smell of food struck his nostrils again. Next to him, Tress remained dead to the world. Rath was tempted to shake him awake to figure out where they were and what had happened while he was passed out. But there was food, and he'd feel a lot better with something in his stomach. If everything went wrong again, at least he'd have eaten.

It wasn't until he was out of bed that he realized he was wearing breeches that didn't belong to him. His were made of cheap fabric and heavily patched. These were good wool, the stitching so fine he could barely see it, and they fit better than anything he'd ever worn, though they were still a bit loose and just a touch too short.

Sitting at the table, he filled his plate and ate—more

slowly than he wanted, but he wasn't entirely stupid—through the food. Soup, fresh bread, some sort of roasted bird… a bowl of mushrooms he shoved to the far end of the table. He'd just poured some wine when a soft groan came from the bed.

Tress sat up, pressing the heel of his hand to his forehead. He glanced beside him—and swore fluidly enough that Rath laughed. Tress's head whipped toward him, and his shoulders slumped, a soft huff escaping his lips. "You're still here."

"Yes…" Rath said, frowning.

"I thought you'd left," Tress said quietly, sliding out of the bed and slowly crossing the room to join him. "How are you feeling?"

Rath set down the cup he'd just picked up, all the problems between them coming back at Tress's words, the tension that remained in his shoulders. Of course Tress had thought he'd snuck out. "Much better, thank you. Even my thigh doesn't hurt past a bit of soreness. Where did you get the breeches?"

"There was a shop that had a few stray pairs. I know you prefer I not buy you stuff, but the pair you'd been wearing was ruined, and it seemed the least I could do." He looked at the table, then slowly back up at Rath. "I am sorry."

"I shouldn't—"

"No," Tress cut in firmly. "You weren't wrong. I was being a show-off, and I am used to getting what I want, and I shouldn't have said such vindictive things in return. I didn't even mean them. I just wanted to lash out. I sulked for two days before my eldest brother made me tell him what was wrong, and then he practically beat the snot out of me. But I've been busy and unable to get away. Then I saw you by the side of the road…" He fiddled with a couple of grapes, mouth drawn down in a pensive frown.

Rath took several swallows of wine, then began to work on the bones left over from the bird he'd eaten, snapping them in half to suck out the marrow.

"You weren't mugged, were you?" Tress finally said. "Low City wouldn't hurt their own."

"Ha!" Rath said. "Even in Low City we have divides. That West End healer wouldn't have treated East End trash like me if not for you. Are you saying High City doesn't have its own divides and feuds?"

Tress made a face. "True enough. I don't think you were mugged, all the same. Muggers punch and grab, and you were hurt far too badly for a simple mugging. I was mugged twice, and nearly thrice, before I learned how to walk around down here without proclaiming that I'm a spoiled rich brat."

"You definitely still proclaim 'spoiled rich brat'."

"Quietly state, maybe," Tress said, scowling. "I don't *proclaim* it."

Rath laughed and leaned across the table to steal one of the grapes. He popped it in his mouth and chased it with more wine. Wiping his mouth with a napkin, he said, "No, I wasn't mugged, although they did take my money when they were done. It was a warning, but it doesn't matter, because soon I'll be out of the tournament and back to my normal life, and nobody will have to warn me about anything."

"Out of the tournament? Why do you think you're going to lose? You're the sec—you're in the most difficult bracket. Obviously, you stand a good chance."

"Ha!" Rath replied. "I still don't know why I'm in the royal competition. Do you know how hard they're all probably laughing in the pub right now? Me, married to a prince. As if they'd ever let that happen." He took a swallow of wine. Tress frowned at him, eyes dark and tight at the edges. "What? I know you said it wasn't as bad as I think, but everyone knows the tournament is rigged, if not all of it then certainly most of it. I was standing right next to the planted 'peasant' who's probably going to marry the prince. Even if I wanted to be in the stupid tournament, it's a waste of time. That's why they call it the Tournament of Losers."

"They're not all rigged!" Tress snarled, slamming a fist down on the table, making the dishes rattle and sending the little bowl of olives bouncing and several of the olives tumbling off the table to roll across the floor. "Some of the families take the matter seriously. The royal family doesn't have some pre-selected competitor in place. They don't! If a family is caught out to be cheating, they're punished severely. Believe it or not, a lot of us do believe in the principles behind the Tournament of *Charlet*." He snarled and filled a cup with wine, hand trembling slightly.

Rath opened and closed his mouth. "Um. That's red wine."

"I know," Tress snapped and took several injudicious-looking gulps. His face soured, and he slammed the cup down. "I hate red wine."

It was the wrong time to laugh, but it bubbled out before Rath could stop it. Tress looked up, the irritation on his face wavering and then finally collapsing into a sheepish smile.

"Sorry," Rath said. "I didn't mean to hurt you… That's what we've always been told. I've heard all kinds of stories about the ways noble houses have cheated. It's High City that first started calling it the Tournament of Losers."

"When they're stupid enough to say it around me, I make them sorry for it," Tress said. "I know it doesn't seem like it, and I didn't mean to get so mad, but there are a lot of us who believe in the tournament and what it's meant to accomplish. Including the royal family."

Rath nodded and nibbled at a few of the remaining

olives.

"So you don't really want to continue with the tournament?" Tress asked. "Even though you've come so far?"

Shrugging, swallowing a bite of olive, Rath replied, "Well, yeah. I mean even if I did win, which is unlikely, I don't think they'd actually permit it. There's commoner and then there's East End whore. Anyway, I don't have any money, I've only traveled out of the city once, and a lot of those other people on stage looked far more qualified than me. Especially the one next to me, in the expensive clothes and smug little grin. You might think the royal family is all noble, but I know a hoity-toity when I see one, and if he's not one, it's only to squeak by the rules." He ate another olive. "What about you, fancy boy? You said you were one of the marriage candidates, right? I'm guessing, given how vehement you are about all this, that your family doesn't have one already picked out."

"I'm not getting married unless it's somebody I *want* to marry," Tress replied. "I may be a tournament prize, but if someone like that smug jerk you mentioned wins, I'll refuse to go through with it. I won't marry someone who misses the point of the tournament—the point of the *law*."

Rath's mouth turned down. "The law says you have to marry whoever wins that right."

"The part everyone forgets is that after the tournament is over, the candidates and the winners get a three-month trial to make certain they'll get on together. It's not simply 'win tournament and go immediately to temple'. If the winner and noble prove incompatible, then one of the runners-up is chosen. It almost never happens, because it is poor form not to marry the winner, but there have been a few instances. I know it's nigh impossible I'll marry for love, but that doesn't mean I have to marry someone I hate. That would defeat the purpose, which is to work together to improve the kingdom."

"I didn't know nobles worked," Rath said, smiling faintly. "I thought they just flounced around High City or snuck down to slum around Low City pretending they're all brave and bold and *different*."

Tress gave him a look that was half-exasperation, half-amusement. "You're supposed to be the mature one here."

"Older, certainly, thanks for the reminder," Rath replied, mood souring a bit. "Never claimed maturity." He pushed his plate away before he tried to eat more. "So where are we?"

"An inn on the West End called the House of Three Sparrows. I've stayed here a couple of times." A quick, sly grin. "When I'm fairly certain I won't be going home anytime soon."

"Your family must be angry you're out right now, given the tournament has moved into the most important part."

Tress shrugged. "No one needs me until the end, and they're used to me slipping away, usually to find a quiet corner to read, but sometimes to go down into the city. They're hoping that marriage will finally force me to stay where I'm told. If that doesn't work, I'm fairly certain they'll move on to chains. But until the wedding ceremony, there's very little they can do."

"Must be nice," Rath muttered and drained his wine. Wiping his mouth with the napkin, he looked at Tress with raised brows. "So what did you have planned for the rest of the evening, my lord?"

"Stop calling me that. I had nothing as solid as a plan. My only thought was to get you to talk to me again. Though I would have preferred it not be because of mushrooms. Speaking of which, I am really sorry about that. I should have asked."

"I should have said, I'm the one who should be apologizing." Rath ran a hand through his hair. "It's too expensive a substance for healers to use on anyone but propers, and temple healers don't give murgot to the likes of me. I get lipseed oil and prayer."

Tress frowned again as he stood. "You keep making it sound like you're a—a monster or something. There's nothing *wrong* with you, and so what if there was? You'd still deserve to be healed properly."

"There's many in the city who'd disagree," Rath said with a shrug. "It is what it is. Stop scowling about it."

The frown turned into a soft smile as Tress reached down and tugged Rath to his feet. "At least if you're being rude, that means you're no longer mad at me. Haven't bothered to read that book of manners I gave you, I see."

"I did," Rath said, the reminder hitting him in the face and making him feel like the lowest for forgetting such a kindness. "I opened it this morning. Thank you. That was far too generous."

Tress shrugged one shoulder. "It was pennies, which we both know is easy enough for me. As I said earlier, I was trying to show off and be impressive. I didn't want you to get bored or fed up with me."

Rath snorted. "It's your lot that gets sick of *me*. Or did you not notice that thousands of my lot showed up to the tournament, and your lot doesn't bother to show at all until after the sorting."

"They're all idiots, because I don't see how it's possible to grow tired of someone I can't even keep pace with," Tress said. His thumb traced Rath's cheekbone. "I mean look at you, competing for the prince and everything."

"Yeah," Rath said with a laugh. "Better be careful

or a prince might steal me away, and then who would call you a spoiled brat?"

Tress didn't reply, just bent his head and brushed a silk-soft kiss across Rath's mouth. Ooh, he remembered that kiss. Hard to forget, even drunk as he'd been. Nobles never wasted time on finesse. They expected everyone else to have it. They were the ones to be catered to, after all, why should they need finesse?

Not Tress. That he bothered to kiss at all was remarkable, and it was so very obvious in his skill and enthusiasm that he enjoyed kissing. The night they'd met, Rath had been amused and charmed, more than he'd wanted to admit. Tress kissed like a sheltered, bookish idiot who'd absorbed a lot of fanciful nonsense that life hadn't yet driven out of him. The same sort of idiot that bought a whore for a night and then spoiled that whore rotten.

And had come back and taken care of him *again,* after Rath had been so mean. For a brief, sharp moment, he was envious of whoever won the right to marry Tress. But that kind of thinking would only lead to madness, so he squashed it and focused on the present. He draped his arm around Tress' neck, drawing him down into a deeper kiss, eager to relearn that mouth, now that he was sober.

He frowned when Tress gently withdrew and stepped away. "Something wrong?"

"You're hurt and still recovering from the murgot," Tress said.

"I'm fine," Rath replied.

"Healer's orders were to rest and engage in as little activity as possible."

Rath rolled his eyes. "That's not even much of a challenge. I'm a *whore,* if mostly retired. I don't need to move a lot—" He scowled as Tress's fingertips covered his mouth.

Grinning, Tress removed his fingers and kissed Rath quickly before darting away. "I bought a new book while you were asleep: old minstrel ballads. If you behave, I may even sing a few for you."

"You can sing?" Rath asked, forgetting everything else they were talking about.

Tress smirked. "Behave and you'll find out."

Huffing, Rath returned to the bed, a delicate tendril of happiness curling through as he slid beneath warm blankets on a soft, firm mattress. Better still was the easy, familiar way Tress settled next to him.

Driving Tress away had been the smart thing to do, and sneaking away would have been wiser than lingering. But the misery of the past few days was still fresh and vivid in his mind, and he didn't have it in him to be smart a second time. He'd just have to handle the inevitable consequences when they came and enjoy himself in the meantime.

Tress could, indeed, sing—at least as beautifully as the temple priests, if not even better. He sang so well that Rath moved without thought, climbing atop him to kiss every sweet sound from his lips. All he got for his efforts was pushed back to the bed and told to behave, but there was some satisfaction to be found in Tress's mussed, uncomfortable state.

Rath fell asleep to Tress singing him a lullaby and gentle fingers combing through his hair.

He woke to gentle shaking and Tress whispering his name. "Hmm?"

"I have to go," Tress said softly. "I am being dragged home on pain of *or else.*"

Rath gave a sleepy laugh. "I am well acquainted with *or else.* I should be going to work, anyway. Thank you, for everything."

Tress caught up his hand as Rath sleepily tried to lift it, kissed his fingertips and winked. "Be well, Noble

Champion. If I can get away again tonight, I'll seek you out."

"Go away," Rath said and tried to swat him, grumbling when Tress moved out of range.

Then Tress was gone, leaving the room feeling empty—and Rath like an interloper. He lingered in the soft bed a few minutes more anyway, before finally climbing out and dressing in the clothes piled in a chair. Some of the clothes, anyway. There were at least three complete outfits, all of it far nicer than anything Rath would ever be able to afford. That didn't mean he wasn't going to keep them. Thanks to those knaves, he didn't have any breeches left. So he'd take free clothes and gladly.

Rath dressed quickly and bundled up the rest of the clothes. Stealing a hunk of the bread and some grapes left over from dinner, Rath headed out, whistling as he wended through the city to drop off his new clothes in his room before he headed to the docks to see if there was still a chance of finding work.

THE SEVEN MERCHANTS CHALLENGE

Rath bought two pies before he headed for the fairgrounds, carefully tucking one away for later in the new pouch he'd bought himself with some of the money from Tress's book. Between those pennies and the money he'd earned working the docks three days in a row, he had nothing to worry about for once.

Well, except the tournament and not getting beaten to death. But he didn't have to worry about paying rent or buying food, which was always pleasant.

He ate the other pie while he walked, licking gravy from his fingers when it dripped. Reaching the fairgrounds, he finished off the last couple of bites as he joined the crowd milling about the grounds.

"Rath!"

He turned and smiled at Kelni, who came up and lightly smacked his arm. "We've been worried about you!"

"We? About what?"

She smacked him again. "The way you were bleeding? You ran out of here the other day like you were going to die if you didn't, ignored all of us calling after you."

Who was 'all' of us? But even as Rath looked, Warf and several other people clustered around him. Three of them were competing against him to marry the prince. "Uh—I'm fine. I was hurt, but a friend helped

106

me out, and since then I've been busy working."

"You're supposed to be focusing on the tournament," Kelni said. "Not working."

Rath shrugged. "What competition are you in? I missed it, and then I was distracted when…"

She and Warf and some of the others laughed. Warf gripped his shoulder, gave it a gentle squeeze. "Your face! You looked like you'd just seen the Fates. I thought you were going to pass out. How does it feel to be in the running for a prince, huh?"

"Like a nightmare," Rath replied. "So tell me already: where are you in this mess?"

Warf laughed again and let go of his shoulder. "I'm with the earls."

"Barons," Kelni said. "Thank the Fates. The rest of them sound terrifying."

Rath scowled, making most of them start laughing all over again. Warf nudged him, though with Warf, that was really close to toppling. "We looked for you at the pub the past few nights."

"I really have been busy or tired," Rath said. Busy fucking Tress or falling asleep next to him, but he wasn't admitting that. Brag about a good thing and it was guaranteed to be taken away. "I don't want to think about how much busier and more exhausted we'll all be once the challenges—" the trumpet of a horn filled the air, "—begin," Rath finished.

"Royal competitors, this way!" A clerk called out, and Rath bid farewell to his friends before following. The clerk led them across the field and behind the stage. Rath's stomach lurched. Thank the Fates he would soon be done with the whole mess; there was no way he would ever survive the whole tournament. "Once the others have been given their challenges and sent on their way, you will take the stage to receive your first challenge," the clerk said. "Remember: you must complete the challenge alone, with no help from another competitor or someone outside the tournament. If you are caught cheating, you are disqualified. If you fail to complete the challenge, you are disqualified. At the end of each challenge, the competitors with the poorest performance will be removed. By the end of the fourth challenge, only two competitors will remain to face the final challenge. Any questions?"

Rath hesitantly lifted a hand, and when the clerk nodded at him, asked, "What if the reason for failure to complete the challenge is something completely out of our control? Like, I don't know, we're mugged or something like that?"

"Such matters are decided on a case-by-case business."

"Thank you," Rath said, relaxing slightly when the clerk gave him a brief, approving smile.

"How dangerous can these challenges get?" asked one of the others, a young, pretty woman with short hair and dark freckles covering every bit of visible gold-brown skin.

The clerk frowned. "If a selected challenge is considered even remotely dangerous, competitors will be issued royal guards to protect them throughout the course of it. But they will never be more than formality and over-precaution; we have no desire to risk the lives of the competitors. Other questions?" When no one spoke, he nodded briskly. "Then you may relax and talk *quietly* amongst yourselves until you are called to the stage."

Cheers burst from the spectators as the crier on stage said something. Rath caught *Ship of Fools*, but nothing more. He sat down on the ground, careful of the new pouch he still wasn't used to having at his right hip.

He tensed when the fancy one sat down next to him.

"You're Rathatayen."

"How do you know my name?" Rath asked.

The man snorted. "Hard to forget a name that ridiculous, especially when they keep bellowing it."

Rath shrugged. If the man was hoping to rile him, he was going to have to try harder than picking on Rath's name. Everyone in the city had already done that. "Well your name must not be as remarkable because I don't remember it, my apologies."

"My name is Jessa," he replied with a sneer.

"Pleasure," Rath said, but did not offer his hand. "You seem remarkably composed. None of this intimidates you?"

"Why should competing for the crown intimidate me? I have just as much right to wear it as everyone here. That's the whole point of the tournament."

"I guess. I'm just a laborer," Rath replied with another shrug. "That's a little bit different than being a prince. I didn't think I'd get farther than a baron, and in my wildest imaginings, an earl."

"What's the point of competing if you start out setting your ambitions so pathetically low?" Jessa replied. "Aim high."

Rath's mouth tightened. "Spoken like someone who's never had to worry about what happens if you fall."

"What is that supposed to mean?" Jessa demanded.

"You're the smart one, you figure—"

"Enough," interjected the tiny woman that Rath remembered as the first one called on stage. "Save your energy for the challenges, because I promise, you'll need it."

Jessa immediately turned his attention on her, and Rath stood and left, moving to the edge of the stage where he could sneak a look at the crowd. Part of it, anyway. He tried to search for a familiar face, but mostly, it was all a blurry mess. A healer had once said Rath required spectacles, but that was not something Rath would ever be able to afford—or keep affording, since with the life he lived, they'd invariably get broken over and over again.

The spectators cheered again, and the crowd of competitors in front of the stage dispersed in a frantic rush. After that went the earl group, and then the dukes. When Rath's group was ushered onto to the stage, he almost lost his breakfast. That was becoming an alarmingly frequent feeling. Stupid. He had no reason to be nervous, not when he had every intention of losing.

On stage was a single table covered in purple cloth, with a man in ornate purple and gold robes standing behind it, the royal three-headed griffon embroidered over his heart. Whoever he was, he was important to the kingdom's finances. "Most honored competitors," the man greeted. "I am Lord Sorrith, Master of the Treasury, and it is my pleasure to present you with your first challenge, selected by His Royal Majesty King Teric: The Seven Merchants Challenge."

Rath had forgotten the challenges had names. Regent Charlet had devised the first ones alongside several members of the court, and over the years, more and more had been added. In recent generations, they just reused the old ones, modifying them as necessary. He knew some of them, but didn't recognize Seven Merchants.

Sorrith opened a coin purse that had been in front of him on the table. He tipped out several coins and spread them across the table. There was at least thirty marks there. Rath couldn't *breathe.*

"Competitors," Sorrith said. "In the city are seven merchants, and mark well these names: Hamm, Chesterson, Merrick & Cold, Charlethta, Semora &

Remma, Barlow, and Greath."

Rath nearly rolled his eyes; those were some of the most difficult, irritating companies to work for on the docks. All of them worked in High City. A fancy bakery, three special butchers that each only focused on one meat, because rich people expected that kind of nonsense, an ale merchant, a wine merchant, and a cheese and butter shop. Greath practically kept city guards on hand to arrest anyone he thought looked at his wine barrels funny.

Sorrith continued. "Your challenge is to buy the following with three marks: one hundred and ten gallons of wine, two hundred and fifty gallons of ale, two hundred and fifty pounds of fish, twenty-five legs of beef, seventeen legs of pork, fifty pounds of bread, and twenty-five pounds of cheese."

That was enough food to feed hundreds. Somewhere around a thousand by Rath's reckoning, though he was by no means an expert. He was just used to moving it all and overheard merchants and customers bargaining—and sometimes flat out arguing—over the price.

It could all easily be had for less than three marks. How was that a challenge? They were throwing away thirty marks just to see who could manage to be the cheapest? Did they think because they were all Low City and out-of-towners that they were too stupid to go shopping? Fucking hoity-toity. They should try to make a penny last a month. *That* was a Fates-damned challenge.

"You have five hours to venture into the city, locate the shops, and determine the best total cost for all the goods. Once you have determined them, make your purchases, and each merchant will give you a receipt for the goods and a token. Once you've completed the challenge, return here and present your receipts and

111

tokens. The two worst totals will be removed from the tournament. Any questions?" When they all shook their heads, Sorrith said, "Come and collect your coins."

Rath frowned, falling to the back of the line as they quickly filed up to the table to collect their coins. Sorrith dropped three gleaming, newly minted silver marks into his hand like they were pennies. Except they weren't; they were shiny, smooth, *slick* marks.

When they were all back in position on stage, Sorrith said, "At the sound of the horn, the challenge begins."

He'd barely finished the words when the horn sounded, though it was nearly drowned out by the cheering of the crowds.

Rath watched the others depart, hanging back, his emotions a storm in his head and a pile of rocks in his stomach. His heart thundered in his ears.

As a silence fell, he realized he probably should have gone somewhere else to try to sort his thoughts out.

"Is something wrong?" Sorrith asked, drawing his hands together within the voluminous sleeves of his robe—a robe that probably cost several shillings at least. "Some reason you cannot attempt the challenge?"

Rath's temper snapped, and he threw his hands out. "What's there to attempt? Shopping? Do you think I'm too stupid to know how to do that? I'd like to see any of you try to survive on a penny and a half a day! Two pennies, if you're lucky and can get work with Barlow or Merrick & Cold. One penny if you're out of luck and get stuck moving barrels for Greath. I have better things to do with my day than exhaust myself hauling all over High City so a bunch of stingy merchants can tell me what I already know."

And that would *definitely* get him tossed out of the tournament, though he would have preferred to go quietly instead of causing a ruckus like his father.

Instead, Sorrith lifted his chin, mouth quirked, eyes gleaming with amusement for reasons Rath didn't even bother trying to puzzle out. Fates spare him understanding the workings of a noble's mind. "Already know, is it? You know so much, brave competitor, tell me."

Oh, they wanted to put him in his fucking place, did they? Fates bugger them! Rath strode across the stage and slapped his marks back down on the table. "Greath—110 gallons of wine for 33 shillings. Barlow—150 gallons of ale, 12 shillings 5 pennies. Hamm—250 pounds of fresh salo fish, 1 shilling, 2 pennies. Semora & Remma—25 legs of beef, 12 shillings 5. Charlethta—17 legs of pork, 5 shillings 1. Chesterson—50 pounds of bread, 6 pennies. Merrick & Cold—25 pounds of cheese, 1 shilling 2. That's the best price, when you can haggle them down to it. Fates know I've heard it all often enough."

The clerk who'd hastened over at Sorrith's beckoning stared at his papers, up at Rath, then down at his papers again before shaking his head and handing the bundle to Sorrith.

Reaching into his robe, Sorrith pulled out a delicate pair of gold-rimmed spectacles and perched them on his nose. He read over the papers, and the small quirk to his mouth became a full-fledged smile. When he spoke, his voice rang out across the field and spectators. "Challenge exceeded!" He lifted the papers high and rattled them. "Most Honored Majesties, your first victory!"

The horns sounded a victory call that would have normally made Rath smile and cheer and clap for whoever was being celebrated. Except they were for him and were rapidly inducing a panic. "What—?" Rath stumbled back from the table. "I didn't *do* anything except yell at everybody. I didn't go to the shops. I don't have receipts or tokens or—"

Sorrith jabbed the papers in his direction, then waved them about like he was holding one of those silly fans a lot of prostitutes used when beckoning to customers walking along the street. "I am the one who makes the final decision, and it's not your place to argue, unless you don't want the victory."

Rath *didn't* want the victory, but how did he say that when people were still applauding and Sorrith looked so approving. He opened his mouth, closed it again. "I don't understand."

"The challenge was to show competence," Sorrith said more gently, setting the papers on the table. He glanced toward the stands, brow furrowing for a moment and then clearing. He picked up the marks Rath had slammed on the table with long, spindly fingers. "With money, with the items being purchased, with the whole process." He stepped around the table and took Rath's hand, pressing the marks into them. "I admit I did not expect to be taken to task, but that certainly did not work against you."

Rath practically had to bite his tongue to keep from saying that made no fucking sense whatsoever and had his lordship gone mad? He frowned at the marks. "What are these for? Do I still need to go and purchase the items?"

Sorrith gave him a small half-grin. "No. Per the wishes of His Majesty, those are yours to keep. Someone else will be sent to obtain your portion of the banquet purchases."

"Banquet…?" Rath wanted to tear his hair out. Instead, he tucked the coins away before someone changed their mind.

Chuckling, Sorrith replied, "The food and drink from this challenge is actually being purchased on His

Majesty's funds to host an end of tournament banquet. It's only a small measure of the food that will be available, but it makes for a good challenge while attending chores."

"You're making the competitors run errands."

"Just for this challenge," Sorrith said. He waved an arm toward the tents and tables off to the side. "Now, you have a few hours before the others will return. Go enjoy food and drink. I promise the next challenge will not be so easy, so savor your leisure while you can. And very well met, Master Rathatayen."

Master Rathatayen, ugh. He could go the rest of his life without hearing himself called something so stupid and not enough time would have passed. "Many thanks, my lord. I apologize for yelling at you."

Sorrith patted his shoulder. "Nonsense, no apology required. Good day to you."

"Good day, my lord," Rath replied and gladly fled the stage in search of that promised wine.

He sat down under the blue tent, relieved to be away from the staring and the touching and the kind of nonsense that caused someone to call him *Master Rathatayen.* His mother would spit her tea laughing.

Rath smiled as he thought about his mother, who would probably cry from excitement when he gave her one of the silver marks tucked away in his jacket. And he'd give another to Toph. The last was all his, and he'd coax Anta to break it down into pennies for him by then immediately paying for several months' rent.

"Would you like something to eat?"

Rath looked up at a woman holding a plate. "Oh! Yes, thank you. I was so lost in thought that I completely forgot there was food to be had. That smells wonderful." Maybe he'd been overly harsh the other day when he'd griped about the nobles not providing suitable refreshment for the competitors.

The woman smiled and set the plate down, then gestured sharply to a boy across the way, who came scurrying over with a cup of wine. White and sweet-smelling, but Rath had no real complaints. "It's not much, but it should hold you until the end of the challenge, and there's some sweets, too."

"Sweets?" Rath asked, looking around. "Really?"

"Really," the woman replied with a laugh as she walked off.

The boy lingered and, when Rath didn't tell him to leave, sat down on the bench on the other side of the table. "How did you do that with the challenge? My grandpa was saying almost no one has ever solved a challenge so fast."

"I don't know," Rath said. "I told them how much things cost and apparently did it well enough to win. Work at the docks long enough and anyone can learn that." He took a bite of sausage that he would never admit tasted far better than the ones made by his landlord. The wine was far too sweet, but it was free.

He sat there eating for well over an hour while the boy rambled on about the tournament and what his father said, peppering the chatter with questions he usually didn't give Rath time to answer. Rath had never been so easy as a child; he'd been too busy working, helping his mother at home, or keeping out of his father's sight. If he'd dared to sit and talk endlessly at someone, he'd have gotten his ears clapped and a list of chores.

How to chat and keep conversation going was one of the hardest skills he'd been forced to learn when he'd joined Trin's brothel. Back then, he'd have been happy to avoid the lessons, but a whore who couldn't talk was pretty much useless.

Eventually the woman who'd given him food returned, saw the boy had lingered, and dragged him off by the ear, blistering it the whole time. Grinning, Rath finally finished off the last couple bites of his food and drained his wine. He definitely preferred red wine. Not that he should have a preference; he needed to stop letting Tress spoil him.

Rath stood and carried his dishes over to a group of people standing by wash bins, thanking them as they took them. Going over to the edge of tent, he stared at the milling crowds eating and drinking and playing games while they waited for the competitors to return. He could see Sorrith among them, the purple robes hard to miss, even if he was blurry. Rath watched him walk a bit, pause to talk, walk some more, pause to talk, slowly working his way to the top where a guard let him through the silk screen that cloaked the royal box.

Rath stared at it, a blur of color hiding an outcome too wild for him to believe it could actually happen. An outcome he should be running from. That he wanted to run from.

Except he'd had the chance to do exactly that, and instead he'd remained.

Because he was an idiot who wanted to die, apparently. He probably wouldn't even make it to the city gates before somebody dragged him into a dark corner to strangle him. Rath turned away from the colorful blur of spectators and tried to figure out how he was going to waste a few more hours of time.

Except in the next moment the trumpets sounded, hailing the return of... A lot of people. He glimpsed Kelni in the crowd, so this group must be part of the barons' challenges. He lingered at the edge of the tent to watch as they all approached the stage and one-by-one, climbed it to present something to the clerk behind the table. Most of them looked wet, a few muddy, as they came trudging over to the tables.

Kelni slowed as she saw him, dismay filling her

face. "Did you lose your challenge?"

"What—um, no." Rath scratched his nose. "I won it, actually. I'm waiting for everyone else to finish."

"You have to tell me more!" she said and dragged him over to a table, where he somehow wound up wedged between her and another woman, surrounded by a sea of faces familiar and not, and was offered more sticky-sweet wine that he really shouldn't drink.

Rath drank it anyway. "Why are all of you wet and muddy?

"The challenge was retrieving some funny blue stones from a small lake in the woods," Kelni grumbled.

"But what if someone doesn't know how to swim?" Rath asked.

Another man shrugged. "It wasn't really much of a lake, more like an overblown pond, and most of it was really shallow. The deeper parts meant those of us who could swim didn't have to fight the crushes in the shallow portions, but that's about it."

"I collected seventeen," Kelni crowed. "Though if any of the other challenges involves climbing, I won't be so victorious. So how'd you win your challenge so fast?"

"I don't know," Rath said, but when that got him a sharp elbow to the ribs, he grudgingly told the story— and got the predicted gales of laughter and swats to his arms and backs.

Kelni shook her head. "Wish I'd seen that. I—" She broke off as the horns sounded again, similar to the way they'd sounded when Rath had been declared a victor. He stood up and strode to the edge of tent, not remotely surprised to see Jessa returning to the stage.

A few minutes later, the victory call spilled across the field, along with more cheering, and shortly after that, Jessa strutted across the field to the tent like ultimate victory was already assured. Which, whatever Tress insisted, it probably was.

Rath was more confounded than ever that anybody thought it necessary to beat him up. "Well met," he said as Jessa drew close and offered a hand.

"How did you finish so quickly?" Jessa demanded. "What did you do?"

"Worked the docks," Rath snapped, withdrawing his hand and turning around—

Jessa grabbed him and yanked him back. "Tell me what you did!"

"If you do not let me go, I will start a fight, and we'll both be disqualified," Rath said in the low, but icy tone he'd mastered taking care of customers who couldn't figure out that he was allowed to say no and money didn't mean they could always do whatever they wanted.

Jessa sneered. "You'll be thrown out for starting a fight, but I won't for defending myself."

"Just who is grabbing who right now?" Kelni countered. "Lots of folks here saw that you were the one to start the trouble. Rath tried to walk away, even."

Jessa muttered curses but let him go. "Tell me how you did it."

"I told you: I worked the docks. There's also the fact I'm *poor*. We tend to pay attention to things like how much food costs."

Jessa glared so hard, Rath could practically feel him vibrating with the effort it took not to haul back and knock Rath off his feet. Not that he actually thought someone as soft as Jessa could hit that hard. "There is no way just working the docks taught you all that."

Rath shrugged. "I work around those merchants and butchers and bakers all day, almost every day. If I wasn't emptying the ships or fetching livestock or grain or whatall from their warehouses, then I was delivering it to their customers. A penny and a half a day, sometimes two, to haul grain and butchered meat and barrels of wine and ale, carts of cheese and bread. Nobody pays any mind to the stupid louts moving the goods, but we have eyes and ears the same as anyone. That's how I did it."

Swearing again, glaring at him with a look so hateful Rath reared back, Jessa stormed off toward the buffet tables that had been set out while Rath was being chattered at.

"Charming," Kelni said. "Who or what is he?"

"A merchant's son, if I had to guess. Most of 'em live in Low City, the same as the rest of us, but they act like they're High City. We call them propers."

Kelni laughed. "We call people who act like that 'city'."

"That's harsh," Rath replied with a grin. He glanced toward Jessa again, and the smile faded, Friar's warning clanging in his head. He should probably find out who exactly Jessa was, and who his family was in bed with. Might slightly improve his chance of not winding up dead.

Or he could have quit the damned tournament like somebody with half a brain. Whatever. He would just lie low, be extra careful, and he'd probably lose the next challenge.

"You look like you could use some more wine," Kelni said. "Come on. I certainly deserve all the free wine I can get after jumping into a lake fully dressed and slogging back here wet and muddy. Shopping sounds like a much better challenge, especially when you're all Master Fancy and didn't even have to leave the stage to win."

Rath pinched his eyes shut, which made Kelni laugh. "Wine is definitely sounding like a better and better idea."

Hooking their arms together, Kelni dragged him over to the buffet tables for wine and more sweets than Rath had ever seen.

Hopefully, they weren't the last sweets he'd get to enjoy.

FOOLISH

He made it back home without incident, but only because he was surrounded by people who wouldn't stop talking to him for most of it. People who kept asking him questions, demanding, some politely, some not, that he recount the story of how he'd won the challenge.

On the other hand, several people had been more than happy to tell what they knew about Jessa, whose grandfather had come into some unexpected money and bought a bookshop, which automatically moved them up in society. If rumors were to be trusted at all, they were eager to keep moving up. A few said they were petitioning to change their family name, but everyone knew that sort of thing took centuries and wasn't worth the effort.

Rath thought a bookshop sounded like a wonderful life. Good money, interesting work, and there were always people who needed books and not a whole lot of bookshops, so above all, it was *secure* work. Who'd want to throw that away on the extremely small chance that a better job could be had? He'd take secure and interesting any day.

People finally parted ways and left him alone as they passed through the city gates, and Rath practically ran the rest of the way home.

Only to be stopped at the door by Anta, who held out a small slip of expensive paper. "Girl left this for you."

"Do I owe you anything for it?"

She shook her head. "No, she said she'd already been paid. I hope nothing is wrong. You've been gone so much lately, and half the time you come back in a sorry state." She planted her hands on her hips and gave him a worried, faintly disapproving look. "What's going on, Rath?"

"Nothing, I promise. I'm just unexpectedly still in the tournament and seem to have acquired a lover, and when those two things aren't occupying my time, I'm busy looking for work."

"Oh, I see." The frown turned into a smile. "A lover, huh? Who managed to turn your head?"

"Just a proper who's taken a passing fancy," Rath said, heart thud-thudding. He'd never mentioned the affair to anyone, his feelings entirely too jumbled and complicated. "For being a proper, he's not all bad. Obviously. Um." He looked down at the note as Anta laughed at him, unfolded it, and frowned in concentration as he slowly read it.

Meet me by the common bridge by closing bell. If you can't, find me at the Harp.

Rath smiled. He should just have enough time to get to the bridge.

A soft chuckle drew his attention. "Oh, the note is from the lover."

Rath laughed sheepishly, ran a hand through his hair. "Yes, and I have to go. See you later, Anta."

"Get along, then," she said with another laugh, shaking her head as he darted off.

His heart kept pounding rapidly in his chest, torn between the thrill of seeing Tress and the dread of what might happen to him along the way.

If there were people waiting to attack him, they'd not yet managed to catch up to him, because he made it to the bridge unhindered. And there was Tress, dressed in dark green and scarlet, long, heavy hair held back with a wide band of red fabric embroidered with green and gold. He looked so glaringly High City, Rath would normally have rolled his eyes.

That, however, would have required he stop staring, and that was definitely not something he was capable of doing.

He was a fucking fool, because even if Tress didn't grow bored and move on, their relationship still had a definite, unavoidable end. He should have held firm after driving Tress away.

Not a bit of that common sense held strong as he reached Tress and was drawn in close for a brief kiss. "Hello, Royal Competitor."

Rath wrinkled his nose. "Don't call me that."

Tress's grin just widened. "Oh, no, you don't get to say that. You said you were going to quit, and here you are still in the tournament."

"I *tried* to quit. Usually being rude to important people is a good way to get thrown out of anything. How was I supposed to know he was the only powerful figure in existence who wouldn't punish me for it?"

"I'm pretty sure he's always been considered eccentric," Tress said. "He's in charge of the kingdom's finances and loves numbers more than anything else in the world. The way you rattled them off like that—"

"You *were* there!" Rath said, brightening. "I looked for you, but I didn't see you anywhere."

Tress rolled his eyes. "Of course I was there. Even if I didn't want to attend, my father would drag me there on pain of *or else*, which is vastly more ominous a threat than death. I prefer to stay out of sight, though. I'm enough of a recluse that most people wouldn't recognize me, but there's always someone who does, and then I get stuck socializing incessantly." He grinned. "Can't have that when there is something else

I'd much rather be doing."

"You're a spoiled brat," Rath replied, fingers moving over the soft material of Tress's utterly ridiculous jacket. It must have cost at least a mark, with all that embroidery. He couldn't stop touching it, wanted to roll around on a bed covered in it. "What in the Fates are you wearing?"

"A weakness to be exploited, clearly," Tress said with a chuckle, capturing his hands and lifting them to kiss Rath's fingers. He smiled happily, as free and open as only children and spoiled idiots could be, but Rath was incapable of not smiling back, which just made Tress smile more. "It's called velvet, and it has to do with something I wanted to ask you. Would you be willing to go along with me on an adventure this evening? I brought you a change of clothes if you didn't want to risk mussing those, since I know you've another challenge tomorrow and do not have several scores of servants to wash and repair everything."

Rath rolled his eyes, but his smile never faltered. "Yes, only one score of servants for poor me. What sort of adventure?"

"A small house party."

"Small house party," Rath repeated. "You're not supposed to be spending time with me, and you want to go to a house party?"

"That won't be a problem," Tress said with a mischievous little smile. "So will you come?"

"When you say small, do you mean my idea of small or your idea of small?" Rath asked, because he had a sneaking suspicion they were not going to agree on what that word meant.

Tress seemed to realize the same. "Umm... not more than two hundred."

"No," Rath replied, recoiling. "I don't know how to do any of that sort of dancing and whatever else you

125

do. That's for *your* lot."

"And *your* lot if you win the tournament," Tress snapped. "We're not all evil and lazy and useless. You spend your nights drinking at the bar. We have parties. It's not that much different. But fine, forget it, we can do something else." He bent and picked up the satchel that had been resting against his legs and swung it over his shoulder, face expressionless save for the tightness around his mouth. He didn't quite look at Rath as they started walking. "What would you like to do? We could grab a bite to eat at a pub or rent a room for the night and eat in."

Rath tamped down on his racing nerves. If he could yell at the Master of the Treasury on stage in front of everyone then he could suffer through a party for a few hours. "Well, we're going to need to rent a room anyway, because I'm not changing my clothes here on the street."

Tress stopped midstride and turned back, regarded him with a mix of hope and wariness. "We don't have to go. I know you hate anything related to High City."

"Not everything," Rath said quietly, heart starting to pound frantically again. "There's this spoiled brat I can't seem to get rid of. I even tried once, but he came right back, like a stray puppy."

"I am not a *stray puppy*," Tress said with mock affront. "Come on. I actually secured a room for the night earlier today so we don't have to wander far after we're done." He dragged Rath onto the bridge, holding fast to his hand, and began to ramble on about the house party they would be attending. Hosted by a merchant to celebrate his daughter's recent betrothal, the kind of festivity that always brought people—invited and not—in droves for the chance at free food and drink.

From all the things Tress was carefully not saying, Rath suspected they were going to be the 'not invited' type of guest. "We're sneaking into a party. Is this your idea of illicit behavior? Would you have a fit of conscience if you, say, had to cut a purse?"

Tress rolled his eyes. "I'll have you know I once stole two marks from my father. He'd told me I couldn't go to a fair, so I was determined to go by myself. He'd left a bag of coins in his desk so I stole two marks from it."

"Oooh, you little thief. Let me guess, the room was empty and he never noticed."

"Stuff it," Tress retorted.

Rath laughed so hard he had to cling to Tress to keep from falling over. "Brave thief! What did you do with your ill-gotten gains?"

"I snuck them back in the next day because I felt bad about taking them," Tress said with a sigh, forcing Rath to come to a complete stop because he was laughing so hard. Tress scowled and kicked his shin. "It's not that funny! And I'm far more inclined to run off with his money nowadays, I promise you."

Rath kept laughing, and harder still when Tress shoved him against the bridge railing and stomped off. Getting his laughter under control, Rath ran after him and grabbed Tress's arm, holding firm when he tried to pull free.

"Let go of me," Tress grumbled, a notable flush to his skin.

"No," Rath said, clinging tighter. "How could I ever let go of the world's most darling retired thief?"

Tress heaved a sigh. "I knew I shouldn't have told you about that. You'll never let it rest, now."

"It's adorable."

"I'm not adorable," Tress muttered.

Rath smiled, hiding it against Tress's arm as they walked.

He'd never wandered through so much of High

City. Normally, he went right to where his mother worked, and the only other time he'd wandered elsewhere had been to do her a favor, and he'd instantly regretted it after all the sneering looks and jeers he'd gotten for being so glaringly out of place.

Tress, still grumpy, but cheerful mood steadily returning, led him to a pretty, two-story building painted green and yellow, marked with a sign and ornate lettering that took Rath a moment to puzzle out: *House of the Three Nightingales.* "What's a nightingale?"

"An irritating bird that people insist sounds pretty, but only people that have never actually heard them," Tress said. "People like to import them to feel fancy, then immediately regret it. This inn had some when it first opened, but they vanished a week after."

"Poor birds."

"I'm sure they were just fine," Tress replied. "Nobody is going to kill something they spent that much money on unless the purpose was to kill it."

Rath doubted that, but Tress was sweet for trying.

Inside, Tress ignored the front desk and simply went straight up the stairs and to a room about halfway down the hall. "Here we are, and by the time you're ready, the party should be busy enough we can slip in."

"You can't steal two slick from a man who will never miss it when there's no one around to see you do it, but you can sneak into a party?"

"One of those is illegal, and the other is expected," Tress replied. "Affairs like this always plan for uninvited guests. If you host a party and don't wind up with at least twice as many people as you invited, the party is an embarrassing failure."

Rath rolled his eyes. "Saying that in a tone of voice that implies it's the most obvious and logical thing in the world does not, in fact, make it sound any less ridiculous." He caught the satchel Tress tossed at him, set it on the bed, and flipped it open. "*What* is this? I'm not wearing this."

"Stop fussing and put it on. I had to guess a bit on the measurements, but it should fit, and I erred on the side of too big."

"It's… too much."

Tress made a noise of amusement, exasperation, and fondness all at once. He strode over to the bed and pulled out the velvet and silk clothes inside: blue hose, a long, tunic-like jacket that was blue on the right side, gold on the left, and sleeves the opposite. It was all so soft, the material smooth and faintly shiny with newness. And all far too fine for him, but he didn't seem to have much choice as Tress began to impatiently undress him.

"All right, all right," Rath said and shoved him away. "Stop that, unless you want to take care of certain problems. You start undressing me, my body expects certain things to happen."

"Later," Tress said with that evil little grin that kept making Rath do things he should have enough sense not to do. Like spend every available hour with someone who was already taken. "Hurry up."

Rath gave him a look. "Patience, stripling." Smirking at the pouty scowl that put on Tress's face, he finished undressing and began to carefully pull on the expensive outfit. Tress's scowl vanished beneath the brilliance of a happy, pleased grin. "So do I look suitably tarted up?" Rath asked, looking down and tugging at the bottom of the jacket, which cut off far too soon for his liking, and he much preferred his breeches to the clinging hose. Erred on the side of too big, indeed. Tress was a lousy liar.

"You look amazing," Tress said, voice gone husky. "I mean, you always look amazing. I was sneaking looks at you in the pub long before you demanded to know why I was sitting there reading. You could be mistaken for a prince easy."

Rath rolled his eyes. "Flattery will get you nothing you're not already getting. Shall we get along to this party of yours?"

"You're terrible at taking compliments," Tress said, not moving when Rath offered his hand. "Why do you think I'm lying whenever I tell you that you're beautiful?"

"Because I'm not, though I enjoy you think so," Rath replied.

Tress sighed and took Rath's hand—and lifted it to his lips to kiss before letting go again. "We're not quite ready." Before Rath could ask, he went over to the satchel and pulled something out. Two somethings, in fact. Beautiful velvet domino masks, one in green, the other blue, both trimmed in colorful feathers and glittering jewels Rath assumed—hoped—were made of glass or paste. "This party is a half-hearted masque."

"Half-hearted?"

"With a full masque, no one is allowed to reveal their costumes to anyone else, and the mask must be full-face. Even the king could mingle and none would be the wiser. Half-hearted is everyone wearing masks to excuse their inappropriate behavior, and while some do keep their identities secret, most don't bother."

Rath's brows rose. "Both versions sound reckless, even dangerous."

"That's the appeal."

"For idiots," Rath retorted.

Tress snickered. "So says the man who took Lord Sorrith to task for making him go shopping. Hold still."

Huffing slightly at the unwanted reminder, Rath held still and let Tress tie the mask in place. It felt strange, slightly scratchy against his skin, and was already growing too warm.

"Now you look all handsome and mysterious, like a secret prince from a far-off land, come to seduce a winsome local."

Rath laughed. "I would say you have us mixed up, but me as a winsome anything is as ridiculous as me being a prince." He smiled and reached out to touch Tress's cheek below the edge of his mask. "You, however, do look all mysterious and prince in disguise."

"Fallen to the charms of a handsome commoner," Tress said with an unsteady laugh as he caught Rath's hand and kissed his fingers again. "Shall we to the party?"

"I suppose we shall," Rath said with a sigh.

"Look on the bright side: parties like this always have the good stuff."

"Oh, believe me, I've kept that in mind this whole time," Rath replied, and tried not show all his anxiety as they left the inn and walked down the street to a house bustling with carriages, horses, and more people than he cared to count. If the space outside was that crowded, how overstuffed must the house itself be?

He faltered as they reached it, but Tress held fast to his hand and dragged him along, and then they were in a mass of drunk, singing, and trying-to-dance people. And that was just the courtyard. Inside the house, things were moderately calmer, but only in that there was an actual space for dancing and the drunks were mostly clustered around the buffet tables or leaning against the walls.

"Here," Tress said and thrust a cup into his hands. It proved to be filled with some dark, spicy wine that was like nothing Rath had ever tasted.

After several sips, he finally made himself stop for a moment. "What is this, and is there any chance I could ever have more?"

Tress gave a soft laugh, and Rath looked up to see Tress staring at him with a smile that did funny things to Rath's heart. "I don't think I've ever seen you so excited and happy about *anything*. You're so easy and willing to go along with my ideas, as long as it's nothing too hoity-toity that will make you uncomfortable. I'm always so frustrated about what I can give you that you'd really, truly *like*, and you're enamored of Hetherson spiced wine?"

Rath's shoulders hunched. "Is that bad? I can drink something else. I wasn't—"

"No!" Tress interjected. "I'm excited. It's wonderful. I hate the stuff, but my eldest brother adores it; he practically keeps the Hetherson family in business all on his own. I'll bring you some next time we meet."

Where in the world would Rath keep wine? It wasn't like his little room had the space for even a small cask. But he didn't say anything for the present, just went along as Tress fetched his own cup of some tart, white wine and then dragged him over to the food tables.

"So this is a betrothal party in High City?" Rath asked, looking around at the milling people, the dance floor where everyone moved to intricate steps he could barely follow.

"Is it so different from Low City? We are all of the one, whatever the divides."

Rath shook his head, smiling faintly. "High City, we're lucky if we can afford a *wedding* party. Who has time or money to host a party simply to announce an engagement? My parents… Well, they never wanted to marry, so I guess they're not the best example. You have a nice dinner with both families, and if the money can be scraped together, there might be a fancy cake or nice wine. That's about it. Wedding celebrations are

132

held in a temple courtyard, since they don't charge for that, and sometimes the ale sellers will sell at a discount for a wedding celebration, so there's plenty to go around. Most of the time, everyone who can brings food to save some of the cost. And we drink and dance until everyone has to go home to be ready for work the next day."

"Ah," Tress said, face falling. "I'm sorry, I keeping making stupid assumpt—"

Rath leaned up and cut him off with a kiss. He tasted like white wine, but Rath forgave him. "There's no need to apologize, and stop fretting. We're at a party; you aren't supposed to frown." He tugged Tress down and gave him another kiss, dragging his tongue across Tress's lips in a way that guaranteed a full-body shiver.

Drawing back, looking much more his usual cheerful self, Tress said, "I'm fairly certain you *are* supposed to dance."

"I don't know how—not this kind of dancing anyway." Rath quickly drank several more sips of wine, because he had the feeling he was going to need the fortification very, very soon.

Tress cast the dance floor an unimpressed look. "Neither do they. Come on." Rath barely had a chance to set his cup down before he was being dragged into the crush and pushed into a line of people directly opposite a line Tress stood in—

And then they were dancing, or something that passed for dancing amongst a bunch of drunk, laughing people. No one seemed to mind that he stumbled as often as he succeeded at mimicking what they were doing. Nor were he and Tress the only ones using every close pass to steal a kiss or mildly inappropriate touch.

Maybe it wasn't all that different from Low City after all.

By the time they stopped, he was breathless from

dancing and laughing, smiling so hard it almost hurt. He went easily when Tress pushed him into a dark corner and settled into a thorough ravishment—or as much ravishing as could be done with clothes still on, masks in the way, and people watching.

Pulling away, Tress grinned down at him. "Having fun?"

"I have more fun when your mouth is against mine," Rath replied and pulled him close again, licking Tress's lips before pushing his tongue in deep, still able to taste hints of white wine, but mostly only tasting *them*. Tress's hands fluttered about, his light touches the best and worst sort of torment. He moaned when Tress drew back enough that he had to stop kissing. "Come back here."

Tress laughed. "No, I want to play some more. How about some more wine and then we can see what games are to be had."

"As you wish, then, but I had better be compensated for my suffering later," Rath groused and went easily as he was dragged once more to the refreshment table before Tress whisked them off to the courtyard. Despite the crush, people were managing to play various games.

Tress eventually decided on one that involved hoops and stakes, betting farthings on who could throw the most hoops onto the stakes. Rath tried a few times and came out of it with two pennies, but mostly he was content to drink his wine and admire Tress. Rath was not the solitary-natured person that his mother was, happy to stay in her room with private amusements or play cards with one or two friends, but he wasn't quite used to the large numbers of people that Tress considered normal. For all that Tress professed to prefer his books and solitude, he was remarkably outgoing most of the time. Then again, they almost always stayed in or did something just the two of them, and Rath didn't think that was entirely for his own benefit or even because they shouldn't be spending time together.

Whatever they did, Rath could happily watch Tress the entire time. His breath caught on the sharp, hard pain twisting in his chest. He'd vowed not to think upon it, because there was little point, but the unhappy fact loomed all the same, waiting for a chance to foul his good mood with reality.

Enjoy it while it lasts was a common utterance in Low City. Because nothing lasted forever, especially the good things. But enjoying Tress while he could wasn't going to make it any easier when he finally lost and went back to his ordinary life, and Tress inevitably drifted away to marry whoever won his hand in the tournament.

He startled when Tress abruptly turned and looked at him, and drew a sharp breath as Tress strode up and grabbed his arms, squeezing gently. "What's wrong?"

"That's what I was about to ask you," Tress said with a frown. "You look so sad, like you did that day we crossed paths after our fight. Are you all right?"

Rath nodded. "I'm fine, if starting to grow a little chilly. You should warm me up."

With a soft growl, Tress bent to kiss him, awkward with the masks, but searing all the same. They were both panting when they drew apart, and Rath did not even care about the ribald comments and cheers being tossed at them. "I think we should adjourn to a private party."

"I agree completely," Rath replied, and yelped as they moved so quickly that his wine cup went tumbling from his fingers to be rapidly lost in the crush.

Back on the street, Tress pushed him up against a bit of wall and tore off their masks, taking a hungry, toothy kiss that made Rath painfully aware that his pants were far tighter than he usually wore them. He pushed Tress back, if with greatest reluctance, and hissed, "You're going to get us arrested for obscenity. Behave."

"Fine, fine." Tress took his hand again as they headed back to their room for the night.

Rath's head was spinning from wine and dancing and illicit kisses. Tress made it far too easy to forget all the things he should be worrying about, made it seem as simple as breathing to banish the rest of the world and focus only on them. On stripping the clothes from Tress's body and kissing every strip of skin he could easily reach along the way. On letting Tress push him down into the soft bedding and have his every wicked way, because the only thing better than sinking deep into Tress's body and holding him close was the way Tress fucked him like he never intended to let Rath go, never wanted to be anywhere else.

They finally collapsed in a sweaty, messy heat, and Rath only grunted the barest protest when Tress plastered himself against Rath's side. "I'm not going to have any energy for whatever they're subjecting me to tomorrow."

"You'll be fine. I have every faith." Tress nuzzled against him. "Just watch, you'll win the whole thing."

"I will not," Rath grumbled, fighting the stinging hurt that rose up. Why was Tress so excited to see him doing well? Why didn't he want Rath to lose? Wasn't he at all upset that eventually they'd have to end their relationship? Did he care so little that if Rath won he'd marry someone else and they'd be driven that much further apart?

Rath cut the thought off with a soft snarl, grateful that Tress did nothing more than grumble in his sleep.

Stupid. They were having an affair, the sort of fun

that was meant to be temporary. As sweet and fun and damnably endearing as Tress was, they both knew this would never last. Tress was probably just happy for him that he might have a promising life ahead of him. Who wouldn't want to become a prince?

Except Rath had no desire to be a damned prince. If he had to start over in a whole new life... he'd rather it be because Tress wanted him there.

But Tress didn't, or he wouldn't be so happy that Rath might win the tournament.

So, fine. He would work harder at simply enjoying the moments, make certain he lost the next challenge, and that would be that.

It was still a long while before he was finally able to fall asleep.

THE HEART OF GOLD CHALLENGE

Rath could barely keep his eyes open. The downside to having an ardent, addictive lover was that sleep seemed negligible right up until he walked around in an exhausted daze the next day. He was old enough to know better, but where Tress was concerned, he seemed to have no sense at all.

He jerked, nearly toppling, as someone walked by him close enough to slam into his shoulder. Rath didn't even bother looking; he could smell Jessa's cloying perfume.

The other competitors had already set out on their challenges, the royals saved for last, as always. Rath felt like a griffon in a fighting ring.

Instead of Lord Sorrith, a huge, burly man with black-brown skin and a long, gray-threaded beard stood before them and boomed out, "Merry morning, competitors! I hope you're ready to work those muscles. Today is not going to be a light day of shopping for you! I am Master Montague, Seneschal of Castle Salvare, and it is my honor to present you with your second challenge: the Heart of Gold Challenge!"

Why had he expected it to be something *less* ridiculous sounding than the first one? What did a Heart of Gold Challenge entail? Who could perform the greatest number of good deeds in a single day?

"For this challenge," Montague continued booming

on, "you are to travel down the temple path to the Faded Temple and there complete the three tasks given to you by Their Most Holy Eminence. Once your tasks are completed to their satisfaction, they will bestow upon you a token, which you are to bring back to me. Remember, competitors—swiftness is not always the most crucial element. How well you perform the challenges, the choices you make, count for much more than finishing quickly. The two lowest-scoring individuals will be removed from the tournament, and the remaining six will continue on. Any questions?"

Rath shook his head, glancing surreptitiously around at the other competitors. They all looked as exhausted as he felt, and most of them looked confused. Definitely out-of-towners, though the clothes had already given that away. He yawned as Montague explained the temple path to those who did not know it.

About a two-hour walk south of the city was the oldest temple in the kingdom. It had begun life as a simple lighthouse to warn ships of the nasty stretch of rocks that vanished completely up around Salvare. Over time, it had become first a small temple, then a great one, then a famous one. People from all over the world came to see the Temple of the Eternal Light of Fate.

Most just didn't know that the way to it was a long, rocky stretch of road simply called the 'temple path' by city folk, though it probably had some official name like The Path of Light. The royal temple in the center of High City was the seat of power for the followers of the Holy Fates, but the Eternal Light Temple, also called the Faded Temple because the dark stones from which it was made had turned pale gray over the years, was the second-most powerful.

It was also, in case they'd managed to overlook that part, a *two-hour walk*. On a good day, when the road

139

wasn't especially busy and packed with foreigners and vendors and thieves and the occasional wild griffon desperate for food.

A few minutes later, the competitors were released, and Rath made certain to walk slowly in front of Jessa, who finally swore loudly and shoved him to the side, then tramped down the stage steps and bolted toward a horse that looked obscenely expensive, even for a horse.

Most of the others were mounting horses as well. Rath and the other competitor from the city were the only ones who would be walking.

At least he was guaranteed to lose the challenge. He waved at the other competitor, Sarie, if he recalled correctly, and then lingered a bit to see if he could see Tress in the crowd. But as before, if Tress was there, he wasn't where Rath could make him out.

Giving up, he let his eyes drift to the ominous silk screen at the top of the stands, heart twisting in his chest. What would Tress say or do if Rath *did* marry the prince? Fates, he was letting his damned affair and this stupid tournament get into his head.

Laborer. Occasional whore. Poor commoner. He wasn't anyone, tournament or not, that a prince—or a beautiful, confounding lord—would ever want to marry.

Turning away from the stands, he finally headed out and began the long walk back toward the city gates, where he could then take the road to the temple, set high on a cliff that made it visible from the highest parts of the city on a clear day.

He paused at the gates to buy food and munched on a belated breakfast as he began the long walk. The ring on his finger occasionally caught the sunlight, flashing in his eyes like some sort of taunt. It seemed idiotic to bother doing the challenge at all. He could go home, find work, return to the tournament in the evening and say he'd failed.

But if he was going to lose, he wanted to lose honestly. That sounded stupid, but the point remained: he wanted to lose because he'd lost, not because he hadn't even tried.

Rath finished off his pie and licked his fingers, fished out a kerchief to clean them and wipe his mouth. Sea air rustled through his thick hair, carrying the scent of salt and sand, clean air that did not smell of even a whiff of city stench or fish.

The road was busy, but not unbearably so, with people heading toward the temple and others returning from it. He picked up a tune from a passing woman and began to hum it, then whistle.

He'd just started to enjoy the walk despite himself, when the sound of crying caught his attention right before someone grabbed him. "Sir! Good sir! Won't you help me?"

Rath turned and caught the woman who stumbled into his space. "What's wrong, good miss?"

"My brother got angry and left me, and my ankle is in bad shape. I need to reach the city, but..." She sniffled. "Would you be kind enough to help me?"

"Of course," Rath replied and reached into his pouch for a clean handkerchief. He handed it over. "Do you have any belongings?"

She sniffled again, nodding toward a small tree and some scrubby bushes where he could just see a worn, faded pack tucked beneath them. "It's over—" she stumbled as she tried to take a step. Rath reached out and caught her, held her close, and helped her over to the tree. Once they reached it, he slung the pack over one shoulder—then shook his head and set it down again. "I'll carry you on my back. That's easier than you overstraining yourself on that ankle."

"Oh, no, I couldn't—"

He cut her off with a wave of his hand. "You don't look any heavier than the crates and sacks I sling around most every day, and your pack weighs next to nothing. Come on, up you go." He pulled the pack on so it rested against his chest, then knelt so she could climb on his back.

"What's your name?" Rath asked after a couple of minutes.

"Brina. You are?"

"Rath, pleasure to make your acquaintance." She didn't say anything in reply, but in her position, he would be completely out of words, too, so Rath filled the silence with some of the bawdy songs they sang at the docks, and she was still giggling when they reached the city gates a half hour or so later.

City guards came rushing over when he beckoned and were happy to help her from there. Rath tried to refuse the little hand-carved good fortune charm she pressed on him in thanks, but at last gave in and, with a parting wave, turned around and once more headed back down the temple path.

He got much farther the second time, at least halfway, when he heard someone crying for help and saw a small cluster of people standing at the edge of the cliffs that had begun to line the left side of the path as the road curved up toward the towering temple.

Frowning, Rath joined the cluster, heart dropping into his stomach as he saw a boy of ten or so years clinging to the side of the cliff. The drop wasn't necessarily fatal, but broken bones were close enough for most. "You all right, boy?" Why wasn't anyone doing anything?

"I can't climb up. I was trying to get my jacket when I dropped it, and I fell, and now I can't climb back up." He looked up at Rath with pleading eyes. "Do you have a rope?"

Rath shook his head. "No rope. Hang on." He shucked his jacket and tried to improvise a rope with it, but it fell a little too short of reaching the boy. He sighed and pulled it back, then removed his pouches, tucked his coin purse into his shirt, and left everything else bundled together by a large rock at the edge of the cliff. Hopefully, nobody would run off with his belongings while he was doing something stupid. "Watch my things," he snapped at the nearest of the gawking idiots. "Or Fates See you suffer the same." He drew a deep breath, then swung over the edge of the cliff.

"Sir, no—" One of the other men bolted over to him. "You should go back and find rope, or hasten to the temple to seek it out. I was about to do the same—"

"You should have done it immediately, not dithered while the boy grew tired," Rath snarled, then started to slowly work his way down the rough, jagged cliff face. He was going to heave up his breakfast. He closed his eyes, took several more slow, deep breaths, and tried to think about anything but the fact he was clinging to the side of a damned cliff.

When he was as not-terrified as he was going to get, he resumed climbing down until he reached the boy. Looked up, immediately felt nauseous and dizzy again. Rethought his original plan. "I think going up is probably a bad idea because there's no way I can carry you without both of us falling. So let's climb down instead, all right? I'll go first, guide you down. What's your name?"

"Yuri."

"All right, Yuri. Here we go." It took what felt like hours, but bit-by-bit they made their way down. Rath's heart stopped when the boy slipped, and it didn't really calm down even when he stabilized.

Then Rath slipped, and terror filled him, so cold and sharp that it drove out everything else—

And he landed on his back in the sand, hard enough to knock the wind right out of him. When he could finally draw a shuddering breath, he gingerly tested his limbs, eyes stinging with relief when everything worked properly, and the worst he seemed to have was a sore back. Standing, he finished guiding Yuri down.

"All right, let's walk along the beach until we can climb back up to the path without either of us risking death."

Yuri nodded, wiping tears from his eyes before he threw himself at Rath and held him tightly. Rath hugged him back, hoping his own trembling wasn't apparent. "Come on, let's get moving. I'm sure people are worried sick about you." Even if they hadn't been worried enough to *do* anything.

By the time they found a spot to climb up and then hiked back to where Rath had left his belongings, the other people were gone. Rath wasn't at all surprised to see his belongings were gone as well. His pouches, his lunch, his newly-bought handkerchiefs—thank the Fates he hadn't carried anything valuable with him today and his coins were safely tucked inside his shirt.

Still, the jacket alone would be costly to replace, never mind the pouch he'd just bought and the old one he'd had for years and been rather fond of. Stifling a sigh, he turned to the boy. "Where is your family? Isn't anyone traveling with you?"

Yuri nodded. "My brother. He ran back to get a rope, but that was ages ago—"

"Yuri! Yuri!" A young man came rushing up, wearing a guard's uniform. "Thank the Fates, you're all right." He hugged Yuri tightly, kissed his brow and the top of his head over and over until Yuri finally shoved him away in disgust. "Are you well?"

"I'm fine," Yuri said. "Rath saved me."

"Rath—" The guard's eyes flicked to Rath, widened, then dropped to his ring. Looking back up, he said, "You're a competitor."

Rath nodded. "Yes, and as happy as I was to help and that Yuri is well, I should be on my way now."

"You have to let us repay—"

"Not at all," Rath said, shaking his head. "Though if you see some bastard wearing a brown jacket with blue and red patches at the elbows, it belongs to me, and I want it back. Fates bless your path, be well." He walked off before they could delay him further, half-tempted to just give up and go back and declare his defeat.

But the day was already too far gone to find work, and there was no certainty he'd be able to see Tress again, so he may as well at least *try* to finish the challenge.

Hopefully without losing anymore of his damned belongings. Rath shoved the thought aside, because if he dwelt on it, he'd be in a foul mood for days.

He hadn't gone much farther along the path when he was stopped again, this time by a woman who was tired and hungry. Rath used some money to buy her food and drink at one of the carts, then headed out once more.

The next person to stop him was an old man who could barely walk and had broken his cane. Rath helped him the rest of the way to the temple, where priests came forward to take over.

"You look exhausted yourself," said one with a soft smile. "Come, I'll see you're well-fed and given a bed. You can stay the night and leave tomorrow."

Rath shook his head. "That sounds wonderful, and I appreciate your kind offer, Priest, but I am here to see

Their Most Holy Eminence for my tournament challenge."

"Oh!" The priest's eyes fell on Rath's hand. "I did not see your ring. I thought all the competitors had long since come and gone. This way, please, Most Holy will be happy to see you."

"Thank you," Rath replied, and followed the priest through the beautiful temple. Outside, it was impressive, but not much different from the city temples, the only difference being the dark stone that sun and salt had turned pale gray. Inside, however, it was white and gleaming, with beautiful, colorful statues of the three Holy Fates in the center of the open sanctuary, where people could gather around it all hours of the day and night to pray, seek solace, or simply find respite. Fate lines decorated every surface, weaving into intricate patterns on the columns and a few patches of wall.

There were statues of the saints in every nook and cranny, elaborate tapestries on the walls, beautiful colored glass in almost every window. Some of the walls were covered in fancy gold writing, while others had pictures that helped tell the stories for people who couldn't read.

The priest led him down a long, wide hallway full of the colored-glass windows, and into a room with a blue tile floor and walls scattered with rugs and tapestries to help keep back some of the chill. A stately-looking person sat at a table covered in papers and books. A beautiful map hung on the wall behind them. Rath and the priest knelt and bowed their heads; he could hear the person stand and come around the table, the bells sewn into the hem of their long, heavy over robe chiming softly. "Who is this, Merri?"

"The last competitor, Most Holy."

"Oh, I see. I had wondered. Thank you, Merri, you

may go."

"Yes, Most Holy." The priest rose and with a brief smile at Rath, slipped quietly from the room.

"Rise, please. I am Eminence Dathaten, it's a pleasure to meet you."

"It's an honor to meet you, Eminence Dathaten," Rath said and obediently stood. Dathaten was beautiful in that imperious, untouchable way that seem common to all high-ranking priests, gray hair bound in a coiled braid at the back of their head, a heavy silver ring on one hand.

Dathaten resumed their seat, glancing at a piece of paper off to one side. "You are the last competitor to reach me, Master… Rathatayen, isn't it?" Rath winced, but nodded. "What has caused you to arrive so late?"

"My apologies, Most Holy," Rath said, angry that he felt disappointed, because this was exactly what he'd wanted. Out of the tournament, back to his normal life, no more time wasted playing stupid games that would never amount to anything. "I was headed here steadily, but there was a woman who needed help…" Slowly, he explained all that had delayed him.

"On the cliff face!" Dathaten cut in when he got to that part. "Oh, my Fates. Are you both well? Were either of you hurt? Why was no one else helping that boy up?" They shook their head. "Never mind. Continue with your tale."

Rath nodded and did so, though it took him some time as he kept cutting himself off with yawns he could not hold back.

Dathaten smiled when he finished. "You've had quite the day, Master Rathatayen."

"I'm not eager to go cliff-climbing again, and I wish I hadn't lost my jacket, but otherwise it wasn't so bad," Rath replied. He wasn't getting beaten in an alleyway or struggling to come up with fifteen slick.

"Well, I think your first task is to go find food and drink. When you've done that, come see me again."

Rath frowned, but he wasn't about to argue with that kind of order. "Yes, Most Holy. Thank you." He bowed low, then left and went back the way he'd come. In the general sanctuary, another priest directed him to where he could find food.

He'd never been so happy to sit down in his life, and the food put in front of him almost made him cry. He wolfed it down, barely noticing when more was piled on, save to say thank you. Only after he'd cleared the plate three times did Rath finally stop eating.

"You were hungry a bit, weren't you, then?"

Rath looked up, smiled sheepishly at the priest grinning at him. "A touch, maybe."

The priest chuckled and took the empty plate, refilling Rath's cup with pale, steaming tea. "If you need anything else, please let us know."

"Thank you." Rath sipped at the tea, looking around the dining hall at the other visitors. Some were obviously from the city, others from out of town, and others must be from other countries entirely. One woman had skin so pale it was like she was made from snow, and her companion had a pink flush to his skin that made him look like a spring rose. They wore wildly colorful clothing, and there was a fluffy white dog at their feet.

Another trio wore lots of beads and wild feathers, and wildest of all, they were bare-chested. The woman had heavy gold rings in her nipples, and the man's chest was covered in tattoos. They probably garnered more looks than anyone else in the hall, though they seemed unbothered by it. But if Rath were accustomed to walking around half-naked all the time, he supposed very little would bother him.

When his tea was finished, he carried the cup to the

collection area then slowly returned to Eminence Dathaten's office.

Dathaten smiled when he entered and knelt. "Stand, stand. Are you fed and at least somewhat rested, Master Rathatayen?"

"Yes, Eminence Dathaten."

Chuckling, they said, "You wince every time I say that. Do you not enjoy being named after one of our most beloved saints?"

"I am honored to be bestowed such a noble name," Rath replied. It was long and obnoxious and who wanted to be named after the Saint of Romantic Fate? He'd been born during the holy week celebrating Sacred Temina and the Saints of Temina, though. It was called the Celebration of Loving Fate, and even his Counter-Fate mother had not been able to resist what she called the sweet charm of it. The idiocy of it, if anyone asked Rath, which no one ever did, of course. "But I confess, Most Holy, that I prefer 'Rath' to my full name."

They laughed again. "Master Rath it is, then. I'm sure you would like to get on with your day, so your second task is this: find my priest Nella and have them take you to the collections; pick out whatever you like to replace what you've lost."

Rath frowned, but bowed and said, "Yes, Most Holy."

It took him a few minutes to find Nella, a pretty priest with a serious demeanor, but who showed Rath to 'collections', whatever that was, without fuss. Unlocking the door, Nella motioned Rath inside, then opened the shuttered windows. "This is where we store all the belongings that visitors leave behind. Two or three times a year, we take it all into the city for the temples there to hand out to the poor. We'll be doing that in another month or two. Take what you like. It won't be missed by anyone. Find me when you're done, and I'll lock it all up again."

Alone, Rath looked over the room, at a loss. Why were his tasks to eat and choose a new jacket? Did Eminence Dathaten feel sorry for him and so was doing what they could, since he'd obviously lost? Well, that wasn't so bad a thing, and it was kind of them.

Moving further into the room, which was comprised of a large table in the middle and shelves all along the walls, everything covered in clothes, sacks, even things like books and shoes. There was even a small case, which proved to be filled with jewelry that the temple probably sold for the money, since it would go a lot further that way than simply handing the jewelry out.

He found a pile of jackets and began to try them on, pleased when one made of fine, dark blue wool, lined in red linen, proved to fit well enough. He also found two pouches, one made of fine brown leather, the other of sturdy black cloth, both much, much nicer than any he'd ever owned.

Leaving a couple of pennies in the jewelry case, he once more returned to Eminence Dathaten. "Thank you for the clothing, Most Holy."

"You're welcome," Dathaten said with a smile, settling back in their seat and folding their hands in their lap. "Your third task is to answer this question: if you were to win the tournament and marry into the royal family, what would you do as a prince?"

Rath frowned, shook his head, shrugged. "I don't know. I know nothing about being a prince. I've worked as a laborer or a whore my whole life. What do I know about being royalty? I suppose the first thing I'd do is learn. Past that, it's impossible to say."

Eminence Dathaten nodded. "An honest answer; I respect that." They opened a box set in front of them on the desk. "Come here, Master Rath, and receive your token."

"Token—" Rath snapped his mouth shut and approached the desk, heart beginning that thud-thudding it was doing more and more of late. Even struggling to appease Friar did not alarm him as much as the damnable tournament.

Standing, Eminence Dathaten placed a small, black velvet bag in his hands. "That is your token for completing the challenge." They picked up a small, sealed envelope. "If you will give this to Lord Montague, for me, I would appreciate it. Would you like to borrow a horse to return to the city?"

Rath tucked the bag into his jacket. "I appreciate the offer, Most Holy, but I've never ridden a horse in my life. Isn't helping me against the rules, anyway?"

"You've completed the challenge, and the time it takes you to return is irrelevant. As much walking and climbing as you've done, I would hate for you to have to walk back as well. Come on." Dathaten didn't give Rath a chance to reply, and simply moved around the desk and strode off, hurrying him along with a wave of a hand.

In short order, Rath somehow found himself sitting on a horse. It was *terrifying*, but he seemed to be the only one who realized that, so he held tightly to the waist of the priest taking him back, closed his eyes, and prayed to the Fates that today not be his day to die. He had survived a cliff; surely he could survive a horse.

He expected the priest to stop at the gates, but they kept going all the way down to the fairgrounds—and right up to the stage, at which point Rath wished fervently that he were still at the bottom of the cliffs. "Thank you," he said and mostly toppled from the horse. He winced as he started walking, and merciful Fates, he would give anything for a day where he did nothing but lie in bed.

But he managed it, stumbling only a couple of times as he reached the table where Lord Montague and a trio of clerks awaited him. He pulled the bag and letter from his jacket and held them out to Montague. "I was told to give these to you, Lord Montague. I apologize for my late arrival."

"You're not late at all," Lord Montague replied with a smile. He broke the seal on the envelope and quickly read the contents, brow shooting up and eyes widening to the size of saucers as he read. "Holy Fates," he muttered, glancing at Rath. He gestured sharply to the clerk, handed the letter to him. "Take this to His Majesty at once."

"Yes, my lord." The clerk ran off, neatly leaping up into the spectator stands and dashing up the stairs to the silk screen. After a moment, he vanished through it.

The other competitors turned their eyes on Rath, most of them looking puzzled, Jessa looking annoyed. Why the man hated him so much, Rath didn't know. So far as he knew, Jessa was doing at least as well in the tournament—and Rath had been the last to return, so he was obviously done. Finally.

But the relief he kept expecting to feel at that realization never came. Instead, he just felt despondent, like he'd let himself down. Which just made him mad, because he was making no sense to himself, and Rath wasn't used to being a stranger inside his own damned head.

Montague bent to speak in low tones with the other two clerks, one of whom briskly began writing and marking things on the papers in front of him. After a moment, Montague drew back and held the velvet bag out to Rath. "Have you looked at your token?"

Rath shook his head. "No, my lord. There wasn't time, and it didn't seem to matter much; it's just proof of completion of the challenge."

"Open the bag, Master Rathatayen."

Stifling a sigh, Rath took the bag and untied the knots, tipping the bag so the contents spilled into his palm. His breath caught. Given the title of the challenge, he'd expected a little gilded heart, or something along those lines, but what was inside was a small *glass* heart, cut so it scattered rainbows everywhere whenever the fading light or the torches around the stage struck it. He held it up to catch more light, entranced. Would they let him keep it? His mother would love it. He'd have to see if he could afford to have it made into a necklace for her. Maybe if he did some work for a few days, the jeweler on Silver Street would give him a lower price…

He startled as someone coughed, face burning as he lowered the heart and held it out. "Apologies. It's beautiful."

"Hold it high enough for all to see," Montague said. When Rath had done so, he stepped forward and bellowed out, "Your Majesty, good people, I present the Champion of the Heart of Gold Challenge!"

Rath jumped, nearly dropping the heart. "What?" He could practically feel the glares from Jessa and a few of the others. "I was the last to return. My challenges were eating and picking out a new jacket. I don't understand."

Montague clapped him on the back so hard that Rath almost fell over. Lifting a hand for silence, waiting patiently for the cheering to die down, Montague boomed out loudly enough that the next kingdom over could probably hear him. "A true heart of gold is not one who fulfills a kindness when bid and to his own benefit. A heart of gold is one who is willing to sacrifice his own ends to see to the well-being of others. Though many competitors here today performed their challenges with honor and kindness and diligence, only one stopped on the road to help those in need, though it guaranteed he would lose the challenge." He clapped Rath on the back again. "The token is yours to keep, and…" he trailed off as the clerk came out of the silk screen and dashed back down the stairs and onto the stage. He held out a note to Montague, who took it and quickly read.

Tucking the note away, Montague smiled at Rath and said, "You should know that the child on the cliff was not a task we arranged. The others were, but that boy was meant to have dropped something over the side that would have been easily and safely retrieved. We would never endanger anyone. What you did was very brave, to be admired by the Fates themselves. His Royal Majesty grants you a boon in reward: you may ask for anything in his power to give, so long as the granting brings no harm to another and does not give you an unfair advantage in the rest of the tournament."

"What—?" Rath felt like his heart was going to pop. He wanted to laugh and scream and cry all at once. "I don't *know*. I didn't do anything special. Anyone else would have done the same."

"On the contrary, by your own account there were other people there who could have acted as you did, and they did not. Instead, they stole your belongings and left you to risk your life. Name your boon."

"I don't know what to ask," Rath said.

Montague quirked one brow, gave a soft laugh and slight shake of the head. "Most would be asking for money right now, or jewels that could be sold slowly over time. A shop? A house—"

"I can ask for a house?" Rath's gut clenched. He didn't know whether to laugh or cry. "That's what I want. For my mother. Can I really ask for that?"

Montague smiled faintly. "You want a house for

your mother?"

"Yes. She's getting on in years, and her hands hurt a great deal. She won't be able to work forever, and the teashop where she works doesn't pay especially well. I don't have a steady income. I want to know she'll have somewhere to live, that no one can take away, no matter what happens to either of us. Can I ask for that?"

"Yes," Montague said softly, smile widening. "It shall be so. Your mother will have her home within the month."

Rath swallowed, clenched the glass heart so tightly he was afraid he'd break it. "Th-thank you. I mean, my thanks to His Royal Majesty. I mean, thank you both, yes."

Montague smiled and gripped his shoulder, giving Rath another one of those teeth-rattling shakes. "Stand in line, Master Rathatayen, and let us get on with this tournament."

"Y-yes, my lord," Rath said and fled to the line, right at the far end of the stage, well away from the gawking and glaring of the others, his eyes stinging as he struggled to hold himself together. It was too much, too fast. Had he really just gained his mother a house? He wouldn't believe it until he saw it. Probably wouldn't be able to believe it even then. The whole affair seemed so surreal.

He startled as Montague clapped his hands several times. "Competitors, it has been an honor to host your second challenge. I know leave you in the capable hands of Lord High Constable Quinton, who has charge of the third challenge. Fates see you well."

Applause consumed the crowd as a fierce-looking woman climbed the stage, dressed in the dark leathers and green-and-blue tunic of the royal guard, a sword at her hip, and a gold badge shaped like a triangle with a silver three-headed griffon pinned to her breast.

155

"Competitors," she said, folding her arms across her chest. They were bare, heavily muscled, peppered with blade and burn scars. "I am Lord High Constable Quinton, and it is my honor to host your third challenge: The Weary Traveler Challenge. It will begin tomorrow, but requires some preparation tonight. You will each be visiting three villages, which will be told to you after you leave the stage. At each village, you will complete the task given to you by the village leader. Upon completion of the task, you will be given a token. Those who best perform their given tasks will move on to the fourth challenge.

"Tonight, you are to pack for your journey. Tomorrow, you will gather at the city gates at the waking bell. You will be given a horse, and suitable travel supplies will be provided, along with an escort of two royal guards apiece. They are not allowed to advise or assist in the completion of your tasks, but they will protect you on the journey and ensure you do not get lost or unfairly waylaid. Any questions?"

Fates, he was exhausted already. He had to travel to three villages? How long would that take? What sort of tasks would he be expected to do? But he was too tired and tightly strung to voice any of his questions, could barely comprehend the questions and answers that went on around him.

When they were finally finished, Rath fled as quickly as he possibly could, all the way back to his room above the sausage shop. He paused only to ask Anta to wake him at the gate bell, which would give him an hour to pack his few belongings and hurry to the city gates. Lord Quinton had told him to pack warmly after telling him the villages he'd be visiting—names that meant nothing to Rath—but Rath had little time or money to buy the sorts of costly winter clothes Lord Quinton had suggested.

"You never look anything but tired these days," Anta said as she pressed a plate of food on him, which Rath was happy to take with him upstairs. He ate quickly, then stripped, flopped into his bed, and succumbed almost immediately to exhaustion.

THE WEARY TRAVELER CHALLENGE

Rath stared at the horse as one of the two guards assigned to go with him offered the reins.

They seemed decent for guards. Rath had a checkered enough past that he preferred to avoid guards as much as possible, especially since, until only a few years ago, they'd been led by the most unreasonable, vindictive bastard the city had ever seen. The new bailiff was nice for a guard, always willing to let people go for a minor bribe after several hours behind bars or in the stocks. The old one and his favorite goons had taken far more unpleasant bribes, and usually they were just as happy to be as mean and brutal as they could get away with.

But Teller and Fynn were friendly and willing to chat, which was unusual for guards in Rath's experience. Teller was tiny, barely big enough to hold the sword at his hip, and constantly smiled like he'd heard a joke no one else had. Fynn reminded Rath a great deal of Jen, but friendly, and not one of Friar's favorite goons. She was definitely as big as Jen, which meant she left Rath almost feeling small.

The horse, however, looked like evil incarnate, and he wasn't getting anywhere near the damned thing. "I have gone over thirty years of my life without needing a horse. I wouldn't have ridden one yesterday if Their Holy Eminence hadn't insisted. I'd much prefer to walk."

The guards laughed, and Teller clapped him on the arm. "Walk, indeed. We'd be gone for the better part of the year."

"I don't see a problem with that," Rath said sourly. "I won't have to ride the horse, and nobody will want to kill me."

Teller's levity went out like a snuffed light. "Why would someone want to kill you?"

Rath almost didn't say; he should have kept quiet. That was what he got for not guarding his tongue. But they were meant to keep him safe, and it seemed malicious not to warn them of possible danger. "A couple of guys roughed me before the challenges started, said I should quit or I'd regret it. They haven't done anything since, but they can't be happy I've made it this far—especially after I told them I'd quit."

"Wait here," Fynn said and strode off back to the gate, where Lord High Constable Quinn and a cluster of other guards were talking while they watched the competitors depart. Quinn's easy demeanor was gone in the span of a heartbeat as Fynn spoke with her. They conversed for several minutes, then Quinn looked at Rath, gave a nod, and then turned and vanished through the city gates with the rest of her guards at her heels.

Fynn rejoined Rath and Teller. "Lord Quinn is going to look into the matter and will see that your family is protected. Competitors should feel safe at all times, and we apologize you were attacked."

"Thank you," Rath said. "I'm sorry for the trouble."

"It's why we're here; no trouble at all." Teller's smile returned. "Now, onto the horse, Master Rath. You don't want to lose because you were bested by a harmless beast."

"I'm not convinced it's harmless."

"Oh, now," Teller scoffed and patted the horse's

side. "She's a good girl, this one. Thief, we call her, because if we don't keep watch and make sure she's securely in her stall, she'll wander around stealing whatever food she can."

Rath gave the horse another look. "Really?"

Teller and Fynn laughed. "Really," Teller promised. "Come on, I'll help you up. In a few days, you'll have the hang of it and wonder how you ever lived without her."

Rath very much doubted that, but he surrendered to the inevitable and let them help him up. After a brief lesson, still half-convinced he was going to suffer a horse-related death, Rath and his guards headed out.

Lord Quinn had told each of them the villages they were to visit in private, with strict admonition not to tell anyone else where they were going. They were to visit each village, complete the task, and move on to the next, in the order Lord Quinn had given them.

The only thing more terrifying than the horse was leaving the city. Visiting the Faded Temple had been adventure enough for Rath. Just thinking about not seeing his home for at least a couple of months left his stomach in knots, a gloomy cloud hanging over him.

"You'd think the highest-scoring competitor would look happier about his quest," Fynn said with a laugh, drawing Rath from his thoughts. "What's wrong, Champion?"

"I'm not a champion," Rath muttered, then said more clearly, "I've never been away from home. I don't think I like it."

Fynn smiled. "The homesickness will ease, don't you worry about it. First time I left home, I was stuck on a boat for six months. I cried and cried the first few days. The other sailors teased me mercilessly, but the captain was kind. After a few weeks, I was just fine."

"I spent most of my first trip away from home

getting blinding drunk," Teller said. "Was either so drunk or so sick I didn't have time to miss home, and the rest of the time, I was being yelled at for my deplorable behavior. By the time I eased off the drinking, I didn't miss home quite so acutely. I think Fynn was smarter about it, but she usually is. Don't worry. You'll be so busy with your tasks and such, you won't have time to miss anything. If you want something to occupy your thoughts, just think about how much you're the talk of the castle! Talk of the city, I daresay. Your family and friends must be so excited to know you're doing well. And granted a boon! They say Lord Swinder swooned from shock."

Rath hunched his shoulders and wished he were back in bed. "That sounds like an overreaction."

"His Majesty doesn't hand out boons lightly," Fynn said. "The last time was ten years ago to a soldier, and he asked for a truly impressive number of crowns."

"That probably would have been a smarter thing to ask for," Rath said. But money could be taken, lost, foolishly spent. He'd rather his mother have a house she'd never lose. Fates knew they'd never had that.

"I think it was sweet," Teller said. "Your mother must be excited."

Rath shrugged. "Probably, but she lives above the teashop she works at in High City, and I haven't had a chance to go see her. Hopefully, when I get back, I can visit her in the new house." He smiled at the thought and clung to the warmth that curled through him, easing the sting of the city fading from sight and the unknown looming before him. "How far is it to the first village? Cartina, right?"

"Yes, Cartina," Fynn replied. "Good ale and bread—they have a watermill there that provides flour for the whole area, even sends some to the city. Should reach it tonight, hopefully before dark, but at worst, shortly after. It's the other two towns that will take days to reach. Tremark is about six days from Cartina, and Falton is about two weeks further on from there. The whole trip will take even longer if we get heavy snowfall. We're going to be sleeping on the ground a great deal." She sighed. "Wouldn't be so bad if winter wasn't coming on. Hope you brought a warmer cloak, Champion."

"I don't suppose there is any hope you will stop calling me that?" Rath asked. She grinned, and he sighed. "As to my cloak, this is all I've got. This is my only jacket, too."

Fynn looked at him in horror. "That won't do! We're headed for the mountains—it'll be snowing there. You need proper winter gear."

"Yes, well, not all of us can afford to buy clothes whenever we want," Rath replied, feeling stupid, even though he knew very well it wasn't his fault. "This is always enough to get me through winter in the city. I'm sure I'll manage just fine."

Fynn's frown deepened. "But what about the ten marks you were given at the start of the tournament?"

Rath's cheeks burned, and he stared at his horse as he tersely replied, "Taken by my father's creditors." There was only silence as he finished speaking, and Rath didn't need to look to know that they weren't quite certain what to say. He sighed. "I'll be fine."

"You won't," Teller said. "The mountains get cold enough your fingers and toes will freeze right off. Snow can come down so hard and fast in the mountains around here that you're warm one moment and frozen solid the next. We can buy you supplies in Cartina, and what we don't find there, we'll definitely be able to obtain in Falton." He grinned, winked. "Can't have our champion getting frostbite."

"I am three challenges away from being a

champion," Rath said. "It's ill luck to brag about what the Fates intend. I could fail miserably at this challenge. I must be the least qualified to go gallivanting about. I can barely ride this damned horse."

"Aww, now don't be mean to Thief. She's sweet as can be when she's not stealing carrots. And you *are* champion so far—you performed the best in the first two challenges and did well in the preliminaries. Everyone is excited for you. None of the other groups have such strong, stand-out leads, though to be fair, there's a lot more of all of them."

Rath made a face, but didn't say anything. Even he knew he sounded ungrateful and cranky about a situation so many envied. "If I'm succeeding, the Fates favor me for reasons beyond my comprehension."

"I think more than a bit of skill is involved," Fynn replied. "Come on, I think you've got the hang of riding enough that we can go a little faster."

"We're going plenty fast!" Rath protested and held on for dear life as he was overridden and his horse increased her pace alongside the others.

They stopped for a brief lunch a few hours later, sitting by the side of a large stream that teemed with fish that Rath wished he knew how to catch and clean. Fish was one of those things he didn't get very often, even though the city was right against the ocean, and he hauled the damned things from time to time when the fishermen needed help. His favorite pub sold a decent fish chowder for cheap, but otherwise, he mostly didn't eat it.

"Shall we push on?" Fynn asked as they all finished eating, brushing crumbs from her hands and pants as they headed back to the grazing horses.

Rath groaned at the idea of getting back on his horse, already sore in places he wasn't accustomed to being sore and still a long way from convinced that the horse, no matter how sweet, wouldn't be the death of him. He was too old for things like learning how to ride and questing and freezing to death on mountains.

Of course, he was also too old to do something as stupid as have an affair with a noble, but that hadn't stopped him.

And there was the main source of his misery. He hadn't gotten to see Tress before leaving, had been too exhausted to go out in the hopes that Tress would find him as he always seemed to. Bad enough he'd barely seen his friends and hadn't had a chance to visit his mother, but now he would be missing Tress as well.

They stopped for one more break to refresh the horses and stretch their legs, then made the last stretch as quickly as Rath could manage, reaching Cartina village just as the sun was setting. "I have no idea what I'm supposed to do now. It seems a little too late to trouble the village chief. I suppose we should find a place to rest for the night and speak with him in the morning?"

"Whatever you feel is best, champion. I certainly wouldn't mind a meal and a bed before we go traipsing off to slay a dragon."

Rath laughed, and Fynn rolled her eyes. "There'd better not be any dragons. I'd have to figure out who imported them," Fynn said. "And we'd have to delay the quest to arrest smugglers."

"It'll probably be something much simpler," Rath said. "Or so I hope, anyway. Where should we bed down for the night? I have no idea where to go. This place is so *small*."

"This way, Champion. Follow the sound of drunk people laughing. Those can be found in even the tiniest village."

"I didn't know they could be this small," Rath said. "I can count all the houses, even in the dark."

Fynn snorted. "Come on." She led him down the street—if it could even be called that—to a building that seemed larger than all the rest, with raucous laughter and the smell of roasting meat drifting out. Dismounting, Fynn tied her horse to a post in front of the building. Rath tried to follow suit, but in the end, Fynn had to help him because the knots she used were beyond his ability to duplicate.

The chatter faded into silence as they slipped inside, and Rath tried not to notice—or show that he noticed—the stares that followed them as they took a seat at an empty table. They'd barely done so when a tall, broad-shouldered man with graying brown hair and dark skin with scattered, paler patches strode up to their table. "Begging pardon, weary travelers, but one of you wouldn't happen to be a tournament competitor, would you?" He looked at Rath.

"That's me," Rath said with a laugh. "Are you, by chance, the village chief I'm supposed to speak to?"

"That I am, son," the man said with a grin and pulled a much-folded, smudged piece of paper from his jacket. "What's your name?"

Rath winced. "Rathatayen Jakobson."

The man laughed. "Devout parent, huh?"

"Just romantic and sentimental," Rath said. "Rath is fine, please."

"Well, nice to meet you. I'm Gennis, and if you're not too tired, then I think we can get you some food and get right on with the challenge. We've been having a bit of a village-wide squabble, you see, and when we were approached by His Majesty to participate in the tournament, well, we knew just how to settle the squabbling once and for all." He winked and motioned for them to stand. "Everybody, everybody, the royal competitor has arrived!"

The pub went silent for a beat, then everybody

cheered and lifted their cups, then rose and started moving the tables and chairs around. Several went around the bar and through the door behind, appearing shortly thereafter, rolling out small barrels and stands that they set up against the far wall.

Rath stared as Gennis guided them out of the way. "Um. What did you say the challenge was, good sir?"

Laughing, Gennis clapped him on the back and said, "Why, you're going to select a few ales for us, of course."

"I'm going to what?" Rath replied.

Gennis clapped him on the back again, hard enough that Rath wondered if he was perhaps related to Montague in some way. "The biannual market competition is coming up this spring, and we've got a whole slew of new ales to submit to the ale competition. Only problem is, we've got too many, and the village is so divided between them all that no clear favorites shine through. So, competitor, you are going to select the three ales we'll submit to the competition."

"You want me to drink ale and tell you which ones are best," Rath said slowly. "Is this some village prank?"

"Not at all. Sit, sit." Gennis laughed as he ushered Rath into a chair at a long table that had been improvised from three small ones. The tavern was much more crowded than it had been when they'd first arrived. Tension coiled in Rath's shoulders, and he ducked his head to avoid all the staring.

But it was hard to stay completely miserable as people carried trays full of cups of ale poured from the barrels they'd set up. Teller and Fynn sat to his right, and Gennis sat to his left, rambling through introductions to the various brewers and all about the different components of the ales. It all went right by Rath; the only thing he cared about when it came to ale was that it was cheap and not too sweet.

"All right, then, that's that. Now try the first one." Gennis pushed the first cup toward him.

Rath vaguely remembered being told there'd be food, but he let it go, unable to refuse when so many eager faces were watching him. The first ale was slightly sweeter than he liked, but there was a bit of apple flavor to it that was unusual. "Delicious," he said. "I like the apple." A small group in the corner cheered and shoved and squeezed each other.

"Next!"

This one was darker, less sweet, even better than the first. Rath said as much, provoking even louder cheering from another group. By the time he was done sampling the first, second, and third rounds, he was drunk. They were just getting started, however, and he had to do it all over again, whittling down the remaining six. That left his head spinning and his stomach so full of beer that it had momentarily forgotten the lack of food.

And by the time he had picked the three ales that would go on to the competition, he could barely stand, let alone walk. That was not going to make traveling fun in the morning. Teller and Fynn helped him to his feet, and he thought he heard one of them calling for food. He swayed as people came up to thank him, talk for a few minutes, and say things he barely understood.

He could have wept from relief when he was finally upstairs in a quiet room inhabited only by him, Teller, and Fynn. "That was… interesting." He really wished the room would stop spinning.

"Drink this," Teller said after he'd had Rath sit on the bed furthest from the door. "It'll keep you from feeling completely awful in the morning." He turned to Fynn. "I could string them all up by their damned genitals for doing this to him the very moment he arrived. They couldn't wait until tomorrow, spread it out over a few hours with plenty of food and water? What were they thinking?"

"Eager… to please…" Rath mumbled. "King doesn't even pay much attention to Low City, I doubt he's ever really noticed the people out here. They're probably lucky if they see any sort of royal official. Think how much they'll get to brag if I win the tournament." He laughed a bit. "Unless they lose the market competition." He distantly felt his head thunk against something, but paid it no mind, vastly more interested in letting exhaustion have him.

When he woke later, it was because his stomach was protesting the way it had been treated the previous night. Rath retched into the chamber pot until his stomach hurt and his throat was raw. He stumbled over to the table and sat down, picked up the small hunk of bread on a plate and slowly ate it, chasing bites with some of the strange tonic he vaguely remembered Teller trying to make him drink.

Across the room, sharing the other bed, Teller and Fynn were fast asleep. He hadn't woken them; that was good.

Shoving another bit of bread in his mouth, he wandered over to the window and looked out at the village below. There wasn't much with only moonlight to see by, but he could see shades of the houses, movement of some stray animal darting from one shadowy corner to another. It was so quiet. The city was always noisy, even in the deadest hours of the night and morning.

He yawned and padded back over to the bed, lay down, and settled comfortably, pleased that his stomach did not try to act up again.

The next time he woke up, it was to sunshine and noise. His room was empty, but given it looked to be fairly late morning, even early afternoon, Teller and Fynn had probably been up and about for some time. He hauled out of bed, found his bag where someone had put it at the foot of his bed, and used a basin of warm, soapy water left on the table to wash up before pulling on clean clothes, shrugging into his jacket, and packing the rest. Slinging the bag over one shoulder, he headed downstairs.

In the tavern, practically everyone there lifted their cups or called out greetings, a few playful jibes. "Like none of you have ever gotten that drunk," Rath retorted. "You make the ale. Don't try to tell me you're not at least partially drunk all of the time." That got him several laughs and a bowl of porridge with honey and cream, along with a cup of hot ale that he almost refused, but in the end, it was too good to pass up, even if his stomach tried for a moment. "Thank you," he said when he was done, and pulled out a penny.

"You're paid up," the barkeep said with a smile. "If you're looking for your friends, I think they went in search of supplies for the next leg of your trip."

"Thank you," Rath said again, tucking the penny away as he left the tavern.

He could not get over how *small* the village was. Did they all know each other? Rath knew his own little circle of friends and shops that he saw and spoke with nearly every day, but he knew almost no one in West End, and nobody in High City, except Tress and a couple of the people his mother worked with. It would be strange to know every single person he encountered; no wonder they'd stared so hard at him and the others last night.

The sound of Teller's laughter caught his ear, and Rath followed it around the edge of a small house to what proved to be an open area featuring a large well and several open cook fires, where people were busy baking and roasting food enough for at least half the village. Must be their equivalent of the way everyone in Low City took what they made to the nearest baker to have them cook it.

Teller and Fynn stood near one of them, speaking with the two women watching over the food. Rath headed toward them, keeping to the edge and well away from the fires, and lifted a hand in greeting when Teller saw him and smiled. "Merry morning! How are you feeling?"

"Too old for this nonsense," Rath replied, smiling when they laughed. "Thank you for tending me."

"An honor to assist you, Champion," Fynn said, giving him a playful half bow.

Rath made a face at her. "So what are we about today?"

"Leaving, unless you prefer to linger here today and leave tomorrow."

"Tempting, but I should probably press on."

"We bought you a cloak and some boots that seemed about your size," Fynn said. "Already packed with the horses. We just have to add your bag to the pile and we'll be all set."

Rath frowned. "Isn't that against the rules? You aren't supposed to help me."

Fynn shook her head. "Our duty is to keep you safe and healthy. If you don't have proper equipment when we get to those mountains, you will die. That's no exaggeration. Buying you necessary supplies is no different than buying food and seeing to room and board when we stop."

"It's appreciated," Rath said quietly. Fynn and Teller smiled. They bid farewell to the women they were speaking with, and Rath fell into step between them as they led the way to the stable behind the tavern.

Teller pushed the door open, throwing a grin over

his shoulder. "You look—" he broke off as someone slammed into him, and made a faint, pained noise before dropping to the ground.

The man who'd run into him scowled and looked up, a bloody knife gleaming in one hand.

Fynn shoved Rath out of the way and drew her sword. Rath fell to the ground, face in the dirt, and by the time he managed to stand, the man was dead, Fynn's sword wet with blood. Her face was drawn tight as she dropped down next to Teller. "You stupid bastard, you'd better be alive."

Teller groaned, clutching at his side, blood seeping from between his fingers. "Not for lack of trying on his part, the Fates-rejected bastard. He got me good, but I don't wear armor just to look pretty."

"You could wear royal temple garb and you still wouldn't look pretty, Teller," Fynn said with a slightly-wobbly laugh. "Get on your feet, you sorry excuse for a soldier." She didn't give him a chance, however, simply set her sword aside, got hold of him, and hoisted him up herself. "Come on, let's get you to a healer." She looked to Rath. "Can you help him so I can stand point and take care of anyone else who might come after us?"

"Of course," Rath said and traded places with her, both of them ignoring Teller's grumbling that he could walk just fine on his own. Whatever he said, Teller's skin had taken on a sickly green-yellow undertone, and there was still blood dripping from between his fingers.

Because of Rath. His heart was drumming so loudly in his ears he could barely hear his own thoughts. Someone had tried to kill him, and if he'd gone first into the stable, they might have succeeded. What if they had succeeded in killing Teller? It was one thing to beat up Rath in an alleyway and threaten him with worse, quite another to hurt people who had nothing to do with the matter.

Then again, everyone knew Rath had nothing to do with his father, but they still harassed him time and again, both to get their money and to punish his father by hurting the people he cared about. *Supposedly* cared about, anyway. Rath would have corrected the mistake if anyone had ever bothered to ask or listen to him.

It took them what felt like an eternity to reach the healer, and when they did, Teller was closer to unconscious than awake.

"Put him there," said the healer, a woman with red-brown skin and stiff, curly, reddish-brown hair. She pointed to a narrow bed in one corner of the room.

Fynn hovered in the doorway. "Master Rath, I'm going to take care of the dead man and speak with some people about him. Lock this door behind me and let no one in until I return, all right?"

"All right," Rath said and did as requested once she'd left. He stood near the bed, but well out of the way, as the healer briskly set to work, removing the layers of Teller's clothing and armor, then clucking and tsking at the wound. Rath winced as he got a good look at it: a slash that angled slightly downward along Teller's side, like the assailant had meant to stab, but had wound up slicing instead. A very near thing. If that knife had gone deep like intended, Teller would have already bled out. "I'm so sorry, Teller. This is my fault—"

"Bugger that," Teller said. "The only ones to blame are the bastard who stabbed me and the Fates-rejected shithead who paid him to do it. Stop looking so upset; I've had worse."

Rath shook his head but remained quiet, not certain what to say, anyway.

"Fate-favored, you are," the healer said. "This wound requires stitching, and you will need to stay abed a day or two, but after that, you should be well."

She rose and turned away, mixed something together at her work table. "Drink this. It will dull the pain while I clean and stitch you."

Teller made a face, but obediently drank the unappealing, gray-brown concoction. His expression when he was finished said it tasted as awful as it looked. The healer took the bowl, then sat on her stool once more and set to work. Teller grumbled and muttered but within minutes, was fast asleep. Pausing in her work, the healer glanced at Teller, shook her head in amusement, then looked at Rath. "I didn't even give him all that much. It really was just enough to dull the worst of the pain. Better if they stay awake to let me know if something is wrong."

"You should see what happens when someone gives me murgot," Rath said with a smile. "I'd be out for three days."

"Don't see that much out here, unfortunately." She bent back to her work, sewing up Teller's wound as deftly as any seamstress.

By the time she'd finished, Fynn had returned. "How is he?"

"Well enough," the healer said as she began to clean up. "He'll probably sleep most of the day, which is all to the good. A couple of days' rest, not more than light movement, and he should be fine. The stitches can come out after about five days."

Fynn nodded. "Thank you. Can I carry him back to the tavern to rest there, or should I leave him here? I can pay you for the trouble."

The healer scoffed. "A penny for the potion and stitching, if it's no trouble. I'm sorry for whatever happened. Usually our village is so quiet. The worst we get is some young fool getting drunk and falling off something." She gestured at Teller. "You can take him. Just have a care and see he doesn't do much moving until day after tomorrow."

Fynn set a penny on the little table by the door, then gently scooped Teller up and headed out. "All should be safe now, Rath, but have a care and stay close until we're safely back in our room."

Nodding, Rath thanked the healer one last time, then followed Fynn outside and back to the tavern. "I'm sorry this happened. You're supposed to be over-precaution, I remember the crier saying that. No one should be getting hurt because of me."

Fynn snorted. "No one should be murdered because they're doing well in a tournament they've every right to be in. Stop apologizing and instead be angry that someone dared to try to kill you for no good reason. Come to that, you've been remarkably calm about an attempt on your life."

"My father's creditors have been threatening to kill me, and leaving me half-dead in alleyways, for almost as long as I can remember," Rath said. "It never stops being terrifying, thinking you could die, or that you almost died, but sadly, you still get accustomed to it."

"Yeah, it's not so different being a soldier, but at least we're paid for the pleasure of being terrified," Fynn said with a sigh. "I am sorry. I should have been more on guard. Hopefully it'll ease off the further out we go."

They reached the tavern and headed up to the room they'd only recently vacated. "So who was the man you killed?" Rath asked.

"No one recognized him," Fynn said. "Probably followed us from the city and was waiting until your death could be made to look like a theft or something, since killing us on the road from the city would have looked more than a little suspicious." She gently removed Teller's boots and tucked the blankets around him. "I've sent word to the Lord High Constable about what's happened. You and I can resume the journey; someone will come to watch over Teller and see him home, and another will catch up—"

"Do we have to leave him?" Rath cut in, frowning down at Teller. "I mean, he's injured, of course he probably doesn't want to continue on, but I don't want to simply leave him here alone. What if the wound gets infected? It doesn't feel right to abandon someone who got hurt protecting me."

Fynn stared at him. "You can't afford to delay, Master Rath. The challenge—"

"Fates bugger the challenge. I would rather be certain he is well. I won't abandon someone who was hurt because of me."

Fynn huffed softly, a smile tugging at her lips. "Well, it's your challenge, Master Rath, and to be honest, Teller would be crushed to be left behind. He was the first to volunteer to help with this challenge, and there was no containing him when he was assigned to look after you. But he would take no offense if we went on without him. Everybody I know is cheering for you to win."

"I never thought I'd get this far," Rath murmured. "It's more than a little disconcerting."

"Well, don't dwell on it too much. Keep moving and doing. Don't let the thinking set you stumbling. I meant it when I said everyone I know is cheering for you. If you really insist on remaining here until Teller is on his feet again, I promise we'll do all we can to make up for lost time."

Rath nodded. "Thank you. Shall we go fetch our bags and settle in? I can't say I'm sorry I get to avoid the horse for another couple of days."

"You need to get over your fear of horses, Champion. Don't think because you're staying here a little longer that you won't have to ride—this is the perfect opportunity to practice. If you become a hoity-toity, you'll be spending a lot of time on one, so best get used to it." She laughed at the face he made and slung an arm across his shoulders as they headed out.

Rath eyed her warily. "Why would I be spending a lot of time on horses? The royal family never leaves the city, not that I've ever heard. Even if they did, don't they usually travel by carriage?"

"For one, it's easier to get around the city on a horse. Second point, rumor has it that His Royal Highness Prince Isambard is going to be traveling the kingdom on behalf of the king and queen, visiting all the towns and villages to address problems and simply let the people see at least one member of the royal family. The crown prince can't do it, and Princess Vivien is set to go abroad not long after the end of the tournament. Prince Harrow is pregnant and has other obligations. So it's fallen to Prince Isambard, and whomever he marries will obviously be going with him. Some parts of the kingdom can only be reached by horse, and others a carriage *can* reach but a horse it just easier."

"I see," Rath said. So much traveling sounded exhausting, but not as terrifying as it might have just a day ago. Though he hoped it came with a lot less stabbing.

Holy Fates, why was he thinking about it like it was going to happen? It wasn't. He wasn't going to win the tournament. Staying until Teller recovered was going to set him back by days, and the trip had only begun. His luck had never been going to last forever. After this challenge was over, it would be back to life as usual.

When had thinking that started bringing disappointment instead of relief?

LOSS

Rath laughed as Fynn shoved Teller off the rock he'd been using as a seat while they broke for lunch. "Shut your mouth."

"When have I ever done that?"

"Only reply to that is crude, and I won't lower myself," Fynn replied tartly. "Finish your food so we can get home already. I'm ready for a bath, my own bed, and to not have to look at your ugly face for a few days."

Teller snickered as he resumed his seat. "Please, who do you think is going to be put on watch together not two hours after we get back?"

Fynn groaned. "Stuff it, Tell. If we get stuck on watch, I will throw you in the harbor."

That didn't halt Teller's snickering, but the rock she threw at him did.

Rath shook his head, smiling around the bread and jerky he was eating. He couldn't wait to be home, back to where everything was familiar, but he would miss Teller and Fynn as fiercely as he'd been missing home. Was there any chance he could see them again? But every time he tried to ask, nerves got the better of him, and he bit the question back.

"You don't look very excited, Champion," Fynn said. "Thought we'd have to take away your horse so you didn't go galloping off."

"Ha ha," Rath replied. "We all know me and galloping is a bad idea." He'd gotten used to horses over the past weeks, for the most part, but he still wasn't in a hurry to make a habit of them. "I can't wait to be home, but this was fun, too."

They beamed, and Fynn said, "I'll drink to that, and you can buy them, seeing as you're going to be a wealthy prince soon."

Rath rolled his eyes. "The tournament isn't over yet, and there's two challenges to go. I'm not sure I really want to know what they are. What could be more difficult than traveling around the country for several weeks?"

"Got us," Teller said as he and Fynn shrugged in unison. "I mean, we couldn't tell you if we did know, but they only told us what we absolutely needed to know to do our job for this challenge. Once you hand over your tokens, we go back to the castle." He grinned. "Though obviously, we'll be at the fairgrounds to see you win."

"You're going to be disappointed, then," Rath said. "I can't even tell if I've passed this challenge. Hopefully we're not the last to return." They shrugged again, but their smiles were reassuring and Rath dared to hope he hadn't failed.

He still refused to think about why he had gone from wanting to quit to wanting to win. He'd been drawn into the foolish spell of the tournament, and he had every faith he'd come out a loser. But he was still secretly hoping otherwise, and had no idea what to do about it. The sooner he lost, the better.

"Come on, you lazy things," Fynn said, first to finish as always. She threw the end of her bread at Teller, who caught it and shoved it into his mouth as he walked over to his horse.

Rath went to his own and swung up into the saddle, patting her neck fondly before turning her toward the city. "Home, sweet home, here we come."

The last few hours seemed to last forever, where all the rest of the last leg of their trip had gone by too fast. By the time they reached the city gates, Rath was ready to scream. Instead, he tamped down firmly on his fraying patience. "I assume I give the Lord High Constable my tokens tomorrow, given it's past dark? Should I leave Thief with you or follow you somewhere to leave her?" He hoped it was the latter; he wasn't in a hurry to say goodbye to any of them.

Fynn nodded. "Yes, to the tokens. We'll tell Lord Quinton what time you actually returned and the city guards will confirm it for him. As to the horse, don't be silly, Champion. We'll escort you home and be sure the guard assigned to watch your landlords knows you've returned in case they want to summon additional help."

"That's not necessary," Rath said, wincing inwardly at all the attention and ribbing he would get for showing up riding a horse and escorted by soldiers. "We haven't had any trouble since that one attack. I'm sure I'll be fine."

"Stuff it," Teller said cheerfully. "Our duty is to protect the competitors, and it's our decision what that entails, not yours."

Rath made a face, but surrendered with a nod, giving his address when Fynn asked.

Fynn rode alongside him, occasionally calling out for people to clear a path where the streets were congested. Rath hunched slightly and prayed silently that nobody recognized him. Teller rode a short distance behind them, whistling as they rode.

The whistling cut off as they turned onto Butcher Street and saw a crowd of people gathered around something. Rath's heart jumped into his throat when he realized the crowd was clustered right in front of the sausage shop. He urged Thief to a faster pace, ignoring Fynn's cry to stop. He bellowed for people to get out of his way, finally dismounted, and shoved his way through the crush.

He stopped short as he finally broke through the crowd. The first thing he registered was all the blood, bright and fresh and lurid against the dark, broken cobblestones. The second thing was that it was coming from his father's slit throat. Rath stared, mind blank, heart pounding. He barely noticed the pain of his knees hitting the cobblestones. His vision blurred, and he angrily wiped the tears away.

Someone grabbed his shoulder and Rath jerked away, turned, fell, and barely caught himself on one hand. He stared up at Tomia, the butcher who lived across the street. "They did it moments before you arrived. It was like they knew you was coming and wanted you to see it."

"Who?" Rath asked. Friar? No, this wasn't Friar's—

The tournament. This had to do with the fucking tournament, of course it did. He was *stupid.* They'd warned him he'd be sorry if he didn't lose. He'd taken it to mean they'd kill *him.*

Oh, Fates. His mother.

Rath pushed to his feet, shoving people roughly out of the way as he took off running.

"Rath, stop! Damn it!"

Ignoring the cries, Rath kept going.

He heard the pounding of hooves on cobblestones, but didn't slow, driven by the fear that he'd find his mother dead, too. Everything else in his head was an irritating buzz to be ignored until he knew she was safe.

The noise moved past him, and Rath barely stopped in time to avoid slamming into Fynn's horse. "Get out of my way!"

Fynn dismounted, grabbed Rath by the front of his shirt, and gave him a shake. "Rath! Calm down! You'll get to your mother faster if you get back on your damned horse."

Rath stared at her blankly a moment, but then the words pierced the terror, and he shuddered, swallowed. "S-sorry. You're right."

"Stop saying sorry when you shouldn't, idiot. I left Teller behind to see to take care of the body and the poor guard they knocked out. I brought your horse, which was no easy feat in these streets, let me tell you. Mount up and stay with me. I can't keep you safe if you run off like that."

Rath nodded jerkily and swung into the saddle, hands trembling as he gripped the reins and fell in alongside Fynn. She cried out for people to move as they rode, bellowing much louder and harsher than before when they'd just been taking him home. People scattered like birds, and the few stragglers were hastened away by city guards that had seemed to come from nowhere.

When they reached the top of Low City, Rath headed for the common bridge.

"Not that way," Fynn said, stopping him. "Follow me." She led the way across the massive pavilion, all the way to the west side, where the guard bridge was located. Two guards lifted hands in greeting as they rode onto the bridge, but otherwise, no one reacted to Rath's presence.

Which made sense, since he was with a guard, but he still waited the entire length of the ride for someone to shout at him, stop him, demand to know what he thought he was doing and how dare he.

As they reached the far end of the bridge, however, all his thoughts turned back to his mother, terror climbing right back up to blinding.

"Breathe, Rath," Fynn said. "You won't be able to help anyone if you don't calm down."

"She could be dead!" Rath bellowed, making a

cluster of nearby people jump.

Fynn reached out, grabbed his reins, and forced his horse to a halt. "Rath, you need to calm down. I understand why you don't think you can, believe me. I'm sorry about your father, so very damned sorry. I don't know why they were able to get to him, but if you keep acting like this, then they will be able to get to you and your mother more easily. All right? Now, then, this time of day she's probably still working, right?"

Rath wiped at the fresh tears on his face. "So—"

"If you say sorry again, I will knock you upside the head," Fynn cut in. "Let's go." She let go of his reins and heeled her own horse to resume moving, once more bellowing out clear as a bell for people to move, the *or else* implicit in the tone.

By the time he reached the teashop, Rath could barely breathe. He dismounted and headed right inside, refusing to waste more time by going down the alleyway like usual. Fynn fell into step beside him, one hand resting on the hilt of her sword.

Inside, Rath looked around but didn't see Alia, and he could feel the panic crawling back over him. The crabby old man who usually came to the gate when he knocked came striding up, a pinched expression on his face. "What do you think—?"

"Where she is?" Rath asked. "Get her now!"

The man just glared. "You have some nerve stomping in here. You know the rules. Go to the back gate! We can't have the likes of you bothering customers."

Fynn stepped forward, and the man startled, as if he somehow had completely failed to notice the presence of a royal guard. "Do as he asks, by the king's command."

Blanching, the man turned and all but bolted across the shop to the door in the back.

A few second later Alia came hurrying out, eyes wide. "Rath, what in—?"

Rath cut her off with a tight hug, sobbing against her shoulder, shaking in her arms. Her questions and dismayed reassurances washed over him like a balm. He didn't care what she said, as long as she kept speaking.

Finally drawing back slightly, she said, "Rath, my heart of hearts, what's *wrong*? I don't see you for *months*, everyone who knows us comes up here to talk about the house you asked for, and only *then* did I learn you were in that tournament. Then a guard shows up and introduces himself, says he's looking after me because some people were threatening you, and you show up like *this*? What happened?"

Drawing back, Rath haltingly explained finding his father and what it had to do with the tournament. When he was done, she hugged him tightly again, until he was able to stop shuddering. "Come home with me, Rath. You haven't even seen the pretty house they gave me. You silly boy, granted a boon and you get your old mother a house!" But she smiled, brushed a strand of hair from his eyes. "I'm so sorry, sweet. Come along with me and I'll fix you a cup of good tea. There's some soup left over, too. You can meet the nice guard who's been looking out for me, too." Her gaze flicked to Fynn. "You're protecting my son, I presume?"

"Yes, Ma'am," Fynn replied. "There's two of us, but I left Teller behind to attend your late husband. I'm sorry for your loss."

Alia sighed, looked back up at Rath, and brushed another stray curl away. "Thank you. To be honest, I've been waiting to hear such news for a long time. I am sorry it's part of this whole tournament business. Rath, I'm serious, Mistress Emmi won't mind if I leave a little early. Come home with me and rest."

183

Rath shook his head. "I need to go to the castle first." Rath accepted the kerchief she pressed into his fingers and wiped his eyes and nose. "I'm sorry, I didn't mean to come in such a panic—"

"Oh, stuff it," she said quietly, reaching up to stroke his cheek. "If our positions had been reversed, I'd show you a panic." She stared into his eyes, a frown on her face. "Are you going to withdraw from the tournament?"

Rath nodded. "Yes."

"Rath, no!" Fynn said, stepping forward, her hands curling into fists. "You can't!"

Alia looked at him, face set in that pensive way of hers that said he probably wasn't going to like what she said, but he should listen and obey anyway. "I understand why you'd want to, of course, but I think you should stay your course, Rath."

"Why?" Rath asked, looking at both of them, then away, eyes moving restlessly over the teashop. "I should have quit when I had the chance. It's not like I ever wanted to do this stupid thing anyway."

"That's not true," Alia said quietly, a bit sadly. "You might have forgotten the boy who dreamed of bigger things, but I haven't. He got lost along the way somewhere, no thanks to your father or me—shush!" She held up a hand to emphasize he should keep his mouth shut while she was still talking. "I am to blame, at least in part. Children don't stay dreamers long when they're sleeping in alleyways and temples, though I always tried my best to take care of us. Now I keep hearing how you're outdoing everyone and stand a real chance at becoming a prince, and maybe I'm biased, but this kingdom could do a whole lot worse."

Rath drew a breath, let it out slowly, and shook his head. "I'd rather we both *live*. There are plenty of people who could be a prince, but there's only one of you." He kissed her cheek, hugging her tightly one last time. "Be careful. I'll come see you again tomorrow."

She sighed again but kissed his cheek, patted it. "Get on, then. But don't do anything tonight, Rath. At least promise me that much. If you must do it, wait until tomorrow."

"I'll think about it," Rath agreed, and reluctantly left, Fynn falling into step beside him after bidding his mother farewell.

Now that he was moderately calmed down, everything came crashing down over him like waves slamming against the warehouse during a storm. He was tired. Wrung-out. Distraught. He hadn't loved his father, hadn't even liked him, but he'd never actually wanted the man dead.

And it wasn't just his mother he was worried about. What if they hurt Toph and the others? What if they saw Rath with Tress and went after him? Nobody deserved to die over a stupid fucking crown he'd never wanted in the first place.

"Come on," Fynn said quietly. "You said you wanted to go to the castle, right?"

Rath nodded, pushing his exhaustion away and letting anger take its place. "I want to know how this happened. The Lord High Constable said my family would be protected."

"I am really sorry."

"It's not your fault," Rath replied. "I'm sorry you're still stuck with me, though. I know you and Teller were looking forward to being home."

Fynn gave him a look. "What have I told you about apologizing when you shouldn't? You're our friend. Of course we want to help. No one should ever have to suffer something like that, and we did promise to protect him. Something must have gone wrong. We'll sort it out."

Rath nodded again, mounted his horse, and followed her as they rode through the streets all the way to the top.

When they reached the castle, Fynn led the way around to a smaller set of gates, where a guard stepped forward and held out a hand. "Castle is closed for the night. Oh, hello there, Fynn. Teller just came through— you looking for him?"

"Yes, but first we need to speak with Lord Quinton. Is she around?"

The guard frowned. "I think so. Told Teller the same thing. Something going on?"

Fynn nodded. "Explain later."

Nodding, the guard unlocked the gate and let them through. "Leave your horses. I'll ring for someone to come take care of them."

"Thanks," Fynn said, dismounting. Once Rath joined her, she strode off briskly across the courtyard, bound for a small door at the far east end of the castle.

Rath had been so distraught upon arrival, he hadn't really paid the castle itself any mind. Normally, he would have been excited to be within the castle walls. It wasn't much to look upon at first glance, being made of the same stone and style as the rest of the city. But colorful banners hung from the walls and torches blazed, even at the late hour, casting light across a bailey that was kept in good repair, the stones even and well-cared for, not the broken, uneven mess of Low City streets. People milled about in small clusters, most of them in guard uniforms, but others were dressed in livery or other working clothes.

Inside, the castle was breathtaking. There was stuff *everywhere.* Mirrors, tapestries, paintings, the floor covered by rugs as beautiful as the tapestries. Fancy candle stands, gleaming wood, flames dancing inside colored glass. The smell of wax, flowers, and herbs permeated the place, underscored by fancy perfumes and expensive fabric. Rath tried to look at it all, but between the flickering light, his sore eyes, and exhaustion, mostly it all passed by in a blurry, colorful rush.

They turned down a short hall onto a long one, and a figure sitting in a chair at the end, next to a set of austere-looking double doors, leapt to his feet. "Rath! Fynn!" Teller said and strode down the hall toward them. When he reached Rath, Teller hugged him tightly. "I'm sorry, Rath. That never should have happened."

"It's not your fault. I'm sure the guard watching him did everything they could." Rath had no doubt his father had been offended by the whole idea of being watched by a guard, if not terrified, given how little of what he did was legal. He'd probably slipped the guard's watch the moment he could.

"Come on," Teller said, squeezing his shoulder. "The Lord High Constable is waiting. Fynn, she said you and I should go find out what happened to the guard that was watching him, since she'd like to keep this to as few people as possible until we have a better idea of what happened."

Fynn nodded. "All right. Come on, Rath, we'll drop you off first." They led him down the hall to the doors Teller had been sitting beside. Teller knocked, and Rath heard a muffled voice bid them enter.

They stepped into a large room bearing a table covered in papers and books and an entire wall of shelves filled with more books. Rath had never seen so many outside a bookshop. Sitting behind the table was Lord High Constable Quinton, and she had the ruffled look of someone who'd just spent several minutes yelling at people. The anger turned to sadness as she looked at Rath. "Telling you I'm sorry isn't good enough. This never should have happened, and I'll find out why it did, as little good as that does in the end."

She jerked her head at Flynn and Teller. "I know you two are probably tired, but I'd appreciate you handling this, and once you're done and rested, I'm putting you in charge of safeguarding his family and friends. Don't hesitate to remove and add people as you see fit. If you need help tracking down answers, come see me. Get to it."

"Friar," Rath blurted as the idea occurred to him. "Do you know the Friar of East End?"

Teller snorted. "Oh, we know him."

"A day or two before I was first attacked and warned to drop out of the tournament, he told me to quit before I got into trouble. He might know something."

Quinton smiled, cold and sharp and toothy. "Drag some of our more ominous guards from bed and go pay a visit to the Friar."

"Yes, Lord High Constable," they chorused and with a last touch to Rath's shoulders, departed.

Moving around the table, Quinton pulled a glass and a decanter from a shelf, and filled the glass with a generous measure of amber-colored liquor. She held it out to him. "Brandy. You look like you could use it."

"Thank you," Rath said quietly. "I'm sorry to trouble you so late. I probably should have waited until morning."

"Nonsense," Quinton replied with a scowl. "I'd be breaking down doors and busting in heads if I was in your position. I truly am sorry. I set guards to watch your mother, father, the shop where you live, and a few friends that seemed to be at risk. I even tried to find the lover your landlady mentioned you had been spending time with, but we could not locate enough information to figure out the lover's identity. I'm sorry for that, too."

If Rath told Quinton about Tress, he would

definitely be out of the tournament. But he was planning to withdraw, anyway, and he'd be damned if he left someone at risk for a selfish reason. Drawing a deep breath, he let it out slowly and said, "He's a noble, so he's probably safe. I hope he's safe. If you couldn't figure out who he is, then hopefully no one else can, either. His name is Tress, and that's really all I know about him. I can describe him if it would help."

"Tress," Quinton repeated slowly. "I know the name, actually. I will speak with his family and arrange a guard. My last set of reports said that all was well. I am deeply troubled your father was removed while under the protection of two experienced guards."

Rath shook his head. "My father had no love for authority. I wouldn't be surprised if he shook loose of them and was grabbed soon after that."

"My men are supposed to be good enough not to be shaken loose, and they will be punished heavily for their failure."

"I didn't come here to see that people were punished. I only came to find out what happened and to withdraw from the tournament."

Quinton's mouth snapped shut, and the unhappiness on her face cut even deeper into it. "With greatest respect, Master Rath, I think that would be not just a mistake, but a tragedy."

"A tragedy is a man being dead, not losing a stupid crown I never wanted and probably wasn't going to get anyway," Rath replied. "What does it matter if I quit now rather than lose later?"

"What makes you so certain you would have lost?" Quinton asked. "You're in the lead, you know. All the illegal bets people are making favor you. The royal family, insofar as they are allowed to have favorites, favor you. If whoever is responsible for this thought you were going to lose, they would not have murdered your father to force you out. All you gain by quitting is their victory."

Rath said nothing, hiding in several sips of brandy, then staring at the glass as he rolled it back and forth in his palms.

"Why did you join the tournament, Master Rath? I've watched the tournament practically from the start and have been given detailed reports of everything that's happened since it started. All of them say you constantly show a reluctance and bafflement, until very recently. Why are you doing this if you don't want to?"

"I don't know what I want," Rath said, and as stupid as he felt saying the words, it also unknotted something in his gut, let him breathe a little easier, despite the fear and grief still twisting through him. "I joined the tournament to pay a debt, and then was never able to get out of it." He took another sip of brandy, and then told the whole story, beginning with being dragged out of bed by Friar.

The only time Quinton interrupted was to make an indecipherable noise when Rath mentioned Tress. Rath almost asked why she seemed less than amused by Tress, but right then, he didn't want to know why someone might dislike Tress. He couldn't take one more bad thing happening, especially when he'd give anything to curl up in bed with Tress right then and pretend everything would be better in the morning.

"I maintain what I said initially: it would be a tragedy if you withdrew," Quinton said when he was finished. She took his glass and refilled it. "You've worked far too hard at this latest challenge, from what I've already heard from Teller, for someone who wants to lose and have done. You care about more than winning, which while a laudable goal, is not the only thing that's looked for. I would never begrudge you wanting to withdraw, but I think you should reconsider.

At least give it until tomorrow. We are still waiting for one more person to return and expect them in the next few days. If by the end of day tomorrow, you still want to withdraw, return to me and I will accept your tournament ring, all right?"

Rath nodded. He'd rather hand the ring over and be done, but now that he'd calmed down, he respected he wasn't in the best state of mind for making a decision. "As you wish, then."

"Thank you," Quinton replied. "Come, I'll escort you home, or wherever you want to go."

"That's not necessary," Rath said. "Surely, nothing else will happen tonight."

"That is not a risk I'm willing to take, and after all that's happened, I will sleep easier having attended the matter personally."

Rath nodded, too tired to argue. He didn't really want to go home—he'd never be able to sleep—but where else was he to go? His only options were the street or the temple. Boarding houses would be closed for the night, and he couldn't afford an inn.

Quinton led him out of the room, murmuring to one of the guards in the hall before guiding Rath back through the castle and outside, where horses were already being brought over. One of them had the belongings Rath had left on Thief earlier. They were led by a tall, shadowy-looking guard who exchanged a brief look with Quinton as he handed over their horses and mounted his own. "Come on," Quinton said as she swung up into the saddle, watched as Rath did the same. She gave a soft laugh. "You've come a long way from the man who had to be coaxed onto a horse at all."

"Travel and excessive snow change a mind fast," Rath conceded, managing another bare smile when Quinton laughed. He followed along beside her, the guard behind them, the sound of the horses' clopping hooves echoing across the quiet streets.

It seemed to take hours to reach the sausage shop. Rath dismounted, stumbling a bit as he landed, but managing not to completely topple over. "Thank you."

"Oh, no," Quinton said as she dismounted. "I'm going to examine your room, and the whole house, if permitted, and assure myself all is well." She motioned to the guard to follow them. "Check in with the guards watching this place, get me a report."

"Yes, Lord Quinton." The guard dismounted, secured all three of their horses, and slipped off into the shadows across the street.

Rath went to his horse to remove his belongings.

"Leave that for now," Quinton said. "We can fetch them after I'm certain it's safe for you to stay here."

Rath nodded and led the way around the back of the shop, using the key Anta had given him to unlock the door.

He stopped short as they entered the kitchen, stomach clenching as he stared at Anta sitting at the table, in her nightclothes, with a cup of tea and an expression Rath was all too acquainted with. Bitterness curled through him, but he quashed it. People had the right to be afraid, to want to not be afraid. She started to speak, but he cut her off. "Let me pack my belongings, and I'll go." He walked stiffly toward and up the stairs, stopping twice on the way to rest. He could hear Quinton and Anta talking, but not the words. Hadn't Quinton wanted to check his room? Well, it hardly mattered now, and Rath didn't feel like waiting. He just wanted to get his stuff and go.

When he reached the top, he quickly packed up his few belongings, shoving his hidden money into the inner pocket of his jacket. He looked around the room one last time, eyes stinging. It had been his home longer than any other place he'd lived his entire life. But he knew better than most that no home lasted forever.

Downstairs, Anta and Quinton stood in front of the table, Anta looking down, Quinton's face like a thundercloud. Rath strode up to Anta and said, "I paid you six months' rent in advance. You can keep what you need to cover the cost of removing my father's body—" She flinched, but Rath didn't feel much satisfaction. "But you'll give me the rest back."

Her mouth tightened, but she finally gave a stiff nod. "You have to know—"

"I know," Rath cut in, not in the mood. He understood where she came from—where they all came from. But it never made it easier, never made it hurt less, when he was thrown out because of things that weren't his fault. He'd been a good tenant, and his father was dead, but out he went. She wouldn't even let him stay the night and leave in the morning.

She held out his pennies, and he tucked them into another pocket. "Thank you. Goodbye, Anta." He strode to the door and yanked it open, stepping back out into the dark, cool night.

Anta called after him, but Rath let the door slam shut and walked off. Every step hurt, and his eyes were so raw and sore from crying that he could barely keep them open. All he wanted was a hot dinner and a warm bed. The tolling of the bells, marking the start of night work, seemed to mock him.

"Come on," Quinton said softly. Rath jumped, turned. He hadn't even heard Quinton approach. "I'm sorry that happened. For what it's worth, I blistered her ears fit to leave the Fates blushing. I know a place you can stay for the night."

"I'll be perfectly fine at the temple," Rath said. "You don't have—"

"None of your arguing," Quinton cut in. "You've just returned from a long journey, and the first thing you encountered was your father's murder. It's the lowest sort of reprehensible to toss you out on the street on the same fucking night. You aren't staying in the damned temple; that's barely better than sleeping in the street."

"Wouldn't be the first time I've done either," Rath muttered, but he was too tired to keep arguing.

They rode all the way back through Low City and into High City, where Quinton stopped at an inn Rath recognized from nights he'd spent with Tress. He dismounted at Quinton's urging and followed him inside, while the guard that had been shadowing them was set to tend the horses and bring in Rath's belongings.

A few minutes later, Rath was ushered into a room that had a warm fire burning and food set on the table. How so much was managed so quickly, he couldn't guess, but he didn't much care.

"Sit and eat," Quinton ordered, and went to answer the door when someone knocked on it. The guard came in with Rath's things, and they spoke briefly before he slipped away again. Returning to Rath, Quinton said, "I'm sure you'd like rest and to be left alone, so I will leave you in peace. There is a guard stationed at your door, and I'm leaving the horse for you to use—and you will use it. I don't want you walking. It's too much of a risk. Promise me."

"I promise," Rath said with a sigh.

"I hope you're able to get some sleep," Quinton said quietly, and she squeezed his shoulder in parting before slipping away, the door closing quietly behind her. Rath could hear the murmur of her speaking to the guard again, but he was more interested in eating the bowl of stew and hunk of bread that had been left. He wasn't particularly hungry, but he was homeless and still had to find money to properly burn his father's body. Free food wasn't to be snubbed.

When the food was finally gone, he stripped off his clothes and climbed into bed. He'd just managed to fall into a restless, unhappy sleep when someone gently shook him, whispered his name. Only as he forced his eyes open did Rath register the voice. He stared at Tress's face, familiar even in the dark, voice cracking as he said, "Tress—"

"I'm sorry it took me so long to get to you." He stripped off his clothes and slid into the bed, bundled Rath close. "I'm so sorry about what happened." His hands were soothing as they stroked and petted, comforted Rath in a way nothing else that day had, except perhaps his mother. Rath was too tired to cry anymore, but he trembled for several minutes, clung tightly and soaked in Tress's warmth and steadying presence.

Eventually, when he'd calmed, he drew back and looked up at Tress. "Thank you. How did you find me? How did you even know something had happened?"

"I overheard some of the guards talking," Tress replied. "As to finding you, I've always had a knack for that. I just wish I'd done it faster. I'm so damned sorry, Rath."

Rath laughed, bitter and worn. "I didn't even like him. I hated my father. He was a mean, selfish fool who made life ten thousand times more difficult for my mother and me. But he didn't deserve that. No one does. No tournament is worth murdering people, even if the prize is marrying into the royal family."

Tress hugged him tightly again. "No, and they're fools for doing it—fools who will pay. Did you eat?"

"Yes." Rath's eyes abruptly stung. Maybe he wasn't too tired for more tears after all. "Thank you for coming. You didn't have—"

"Of course I did," Tress cut in. "How could I not?"

There were plenty of people who would think it strange a man did so much for someone he was merely having an affair with. Rath had known Anta for years, had considered her something of a friend, and she'd thrown him out without hesitation. "It's still appreciated. You're always so kind."

"You're kinder by far. Now go back to sleep." Tress said and kissed him softly before drawing him in close again, settling them both comfortably, and Rath finally fell asleep listening to the soft, sweet sound of Tress singing.

THE FEAST OF KINGS CHALLENGE

It took three days for the final competitor to return. Rath and his mother gave his father's ashes to the sea on a cold, snowy day that seemed far too bleak and depressing for a last farewell, even to a man he'd never liked. Then he'd attended the victory ceremonies for the other competitors, got to cheer and scream as Warf was engaged to the second-eldest son of the Earl of Bellowen, and Kelni was engaged to the youngest daughter of the Baron of Diara.

Now, only his portion of the tournament loomed, driving him mad with anxiety as he sat at a table in the room Quinton had insisted he keep until the tournament was over. He turned his tournament ring over and over in his hands, occasionally pausing to run his thumb over his name inscribed inside.

He should give the ring to Lord Quinton as he'd originally planned. But every time he tried to walk to the castle to do precisely that, he found something else he needed to do. His mother's words, Quinton's words, clamored in his head, running around and around.

And of course there was Tress, who told him he should keep trying, that he would be a credit to the royal family...

Why couldn't he be a credit to Tress's family? But that wasn't fair. Tress still had to follow the law, whatever he said about not marrying someone unsuitable. Rath just wished he didn't seem so happy about the fact they would eventually be parting.

Sulking and sighing over the matter would accomplish nothing, but matter how many times he reminded himself to simply enjoy the time they had together, his gloom persisted.

Normally, he would have busied himself with work or spent more time with his friends, but his friends were all busy working, and there'd been little time to work while handling the burning of his father's body, filing the death, dealing with his father's belongings, and then being summoned to the castle to be told what he'd already surmised: his father had slipped away from his guards, and that was all the opportunity the people responsible had needed. When exactly he'd been taken, no one knew, but his guards had been searching for him half a day when he was killed in front of the sausage shop. No one else had known because the guards hadn't reported the problem like they should have.

Rath didn't envy the guards and the punishment they were facing for what Quinton had called dereliction of duty. Summoning more help in the end wouldn't have mattered; his father had probably been grabbed too quickly for it to make a difference.

He was grateful it wasn't his mother they'd gone after first, no matter how terrible that made him.

As to who was behind the murder, Quinton had said she had her suspicions, but so far no hard evidence. If Friar knew, and they'd pressed him hard, he wasn't saying. According to him, he wasn't part of it, just kept his ears to the wind like any half-sensible person would.

Rath just wanted the whole matter to go away.

When he wasn't dealing with all of that, he spent time with his mother at her pretty new house, right in the propers district, close to shops where she could buy food without traveling far and taxing herself, close enough to the common bridge that she didn't have to travel too far to get to work.

And when he ran out of distractions, he sat in his room and brooded—over Tress, over the tournament, over what he was supposed to do.

His mind retreated to the most recent set of happy memories he had: traveling the kingdom. He'd enjoyed that challenge once the homesickness had eased. He'd liked seeing the rest of the kingdom, talking to people, the ale tasting and the pie contest and officiating at the frost fair. If that was what he was supposed to do if he married Prince Isambard, would it be so bad? It beat whoring and laboring by leagues.

He missed his friends and the easy security of his routine. He had no idea how to be a hoity-toity. But…

It was that damned *but* that was driving him to stupid choices, stupid actions. *But* and *if.*

How had the need for fifteen slick wound up stirring hopes and dreams long dead? He was a fucking idiot, exactly the kind of loser he mocked for joining the tournament.

But he couldn't make himself return the ring either.

And he was due at the fairgrounds in a little under two hours, so it was time he headed out. Hopefully nobody else would die or get hurt because he was too weak and pathetic to walk away.

Gathering up the cloak Tress had bought him, despite Rath's protestations that the one he'd bought while traveling was just fine, he swung it over his shoulders and pinned it closed with a plain pin he'd bought himself, despite Tress's protestations.

The guard in the hallway pushed away from the wall, smiling in greeting before stepping in front of Rath and leading the way downstairs and out to the stables.

Snow had begun to fall again, muting the noise of the city and making everything feel soft and lazy. It was an improvement over the dreariness of the morning, at least.

A stable boy approached with their horses, one of them Thief, who had replaced the other horse Rath had initially been given. The boy smiled shyly when Rath gave him a farthing. Swinging into the saddle, giving Thief a pat on the neck, Rath led the way through the city.

He dismounted once they reached the fairgrounds, handing his horse off to the guard. "Thank you."

"My pleasure, Master Rath. Fates See your victory."

Rath mustered a smile, hoping it didn't look as anxious and sad as he felt. "Thank you."

He headed through the open walkways that framed the fairgrounds, strode past the blue tent already filled with people—and yelped when they all cheered and called his name. That set off more cheering and screaming as the people in the stands took it up.

Merciful Fates, what in the world was going on?

Rath almost turned around and fled, but that wouldn't make him feel *less* like an idiot, so he continued on across the field and onto the stage, where the other three remaining competitors already waited. Jessa, Sarie, and Benni. Rath had really hoped Jessa would get lost in a forest somewhere, or eaten by a griffon, but he hadn't put much faith in the possibility. Especially when somebody had resorted to murder to give Jessa more of an edge.

He didn't care if there was no hard evidence, who else would it be? More often than not, the obvious answer was the right one. The Fates-rejected bastard was lucky Rath wasn't willing to risk his standing in the tournament to beat the shit out of him. But once the tournament was over, Jessa had better hope he found a good hiding place.

As the cheering died down, Quinton stepped forward. "Congratulations, competitors! You have done exceedingly well to make it this far. Your Majesties! I present to you the four strongest competitors fighting for the chance to join your esteemed family!" The crowds cheered raucously again, and it was several minutes before Quinton got them calmed once more. "Competitors, be proud of yourselves. Out of the thousands who arrived, and whatever happens the rest of the tournament, you four are the only ones to make it this far and that is no small thing." Quinton clapped her hands for silence.

"Unfortunately, before we move on to the next challenge, there is something that must be addressed. Cheating is not tolerated, and *violence* is most certainly not tolerated. A terrible act was committed against one of our noble competitors, and a life was lost. When the parties responsible for that crime are found, they will be severely punished, very likely with their lives. If you have knowledge pertaining to this matter, you would be wise to share it with me, because if it is found later that you knew something, but withheld it, you will be punished alongside those who committed the act."

Silence fell, and Quinton let it linger for several minutes. Finally, with a minute nod toward something or someone in the stands, she clapped her hands and continued. "Once more, competitors, I congratulate you. Now onward with the tournament, which I return to the capable hands of Lord Montague."

Montague stepped forward as Quinton stepped back, and clapped his hands for silence. "Competitors, as your last challenge was a task most arduous, the fourth challenge will be something more relaxing. Your challenge, to take place this evening, beginning at the closing bell, is the Feast of Kings Challenge. And all you must do is come to the royal castle to enjoy dinner with King Teric and Queen Isara."

That was a terrible challenge. Rath would quite literally prefer to *walk* around the entire kingdom twice. Dinner with the king and queen was the worst challenge he'd ever heard of. Obviously dining with them was inevitable for the winner, but he didn't see why it had to be inflicted on people before they had no choice in the matter. What was the point? It wasn't like they were allowed to say 'this one is our favorite, he should win'.

Which, all right, *allowed* didn't have much to do with anything. But still. What was the point?

"Show up half an hour before the closing bell," Montague said, and Rath really hoped he hadn't missed something else important. "If you have no suitable clothes, show up a few hours early, and they will be provided, but feel no obligation. Whatever you choose to wear is suitable, I promise."

It had damn well better be. But Rath couldn't put much heat behind the thought, not after all the kindness Lord Quinton and the others had shown him. Maybe the lords felt comfortable cheating, but so far as he could tell, Tress had been correct about the royal family being quite serious about the tournament and having no tolerance for cheaters.

He fled as soon as they were dismissed, eager to go and hide—somewhere Tress wouldn't find him, preferably, since Rath didn't doubt for a moment that Tress had already selected his outfit and had it tailored, somehow.

Instead, he went in search of food and settled at a pub at the end of Tanner Street that often had passable food and ale for cheap.

He and his guard had only just started eating when

someone sat down beside him, and his stomach clenched at the familiar scent of spices used in making sausages that always clung to Anta. Rath didn't look up, just kept eating.

Anta cleared her throat, then said, "Rath…"

Reluctantly looking up, he stared at her in silent query.

"I'm sorry about asking you to leave," she said, eyes dropping to the table. "We were upset and scared and thought we were doing the right thing. But it wasn't your fault that happened, and it wasn't right to do that to you, considering you just lost your father. If you want to come back, the room is yours. Only been a few days, but it's not the same without you coming and going."

Another knot in Rath's chest loosened. "Thanks. I'm staying elsewhere through the tournament, but once it's over, I'll come by."

She nodded, smiled tentatively as she slowly looked up at him. "I hope you win, Rath. Everyone was surprised when you joined and we're all so excited to see you keep winning. Fates See your victory."

"Thank you," Rath said and sighed as she walked away.

The guard next to him chuckled. "You look more miserable than when you started."

"I'm just nervous," Rath replied. "Everyone keeps saying they hope I win, but I don't know why, and now what will I do if I lose?" He shook his head. "That's not your problem, though. I suppose I should go get dressed. Closing bell isn't that far off."

They finished eating and headed back to the inn. Tress wasn't there, which surprised him, but there was a handsome new set of clothes on the bed, which didn't surprise him at all. Tress was just being nice, but Rath was fairly certain it was cheating, or close enough it may as well have been. His own clothes might not compare, but even if wearing the fancy ones hadn't been borderline cheating, he refused to show up as anyone other than himself.

All that aside, he needed to start pulling away from Tress. Once the tournament was over, Tress would have to focus on his new spouse. If Rath won, he'd have to focus on learning a whole new way of life. If he lost, it was back to the docks and his attic room. Back to his safe, quiet, boring life that no longer appealed.

And no matter which life he wound up with at the end of the tournament, neither would include Tress.

He shoved the thoughts away before they turned his mood completely black, and stripped. A washtub sat by the fire, complete with fancy soaps and both soft and rough cleaning rags. Rath was uncomfortable with most of the things Tress took for granted, but he would never turn down the chance for a proper bath.

Once he was clean, he pulled on his clothes and the boots he'd gotten repaired and polished the day before. Hopefully, he wouldn't completely humiliate himself at dinner.

Maybe he'd get to see Fynn and Teller. They were so busy supervising the guarding of his friends and family he never actually got to see them.

Outside, he once more swung up onto the patiently-waiting Thief and rode through the city with the guard at his side. They dismounted inside the castle gate, and he left Thief to the girl who came rushing up to take her. Guards pulled open the front doors, and Rath forced his feet to move. He'd much preferred when Fynn and Teller had taken him through a side door the other night.

Benni and Sarie were there, but Jessa was missing, which seemed odd. He seemed the sort to make certain he got all the attention he could, which meant not showing up late. Then again, what did Rath know about fancy dinners?

"Welcome, welcome," Montague said, turning from the other two to smile at Rath. "I hope you're looking forward to dinner. Their Royal Majesties certainly are."

"Of course," Rath said with a smile that he fervently hoped did not show all the panic that he was feeling.

From the way Montague chuckled, he'd failed miserably. Montague motioned to a servant, who came bearing a tray full of cups of wine. Montague picked one out and offered it to Rath. "A little bird told me you'd be partial to this one."

"A little bird?" Rath asked as he accepted the wine. He knew it just by the smell. His chest clenched. "What bird?"

Montague smiled. "Lord Quinton, actually, though she didn't tell me how *she* knew. Enjoy."

"Thank you," Rath said. How had Lord Quinton known what wine he liked? But she'd said she knew Tress; that must be where she'd learned it. But if Quinton knew Tress, then she must know that Rath and Tress had been breaking the rules. Why hadn't Rath been disqualified for cheating?

Well, if no one else was going to say anything, neither was Rath. Maybe it didn't matter because he wasn't competing for Tress.

It was a pity Tress couldn't be at the dinner. Rath would have liked to see him all dressed up in his finery. On the other hand, being that close, but unable to touch or even act like they knew each other…

He took another swallow of wine, as warmed by the memories it dredged up as by the wine itself. Taking a few more sips, he went to join the others and chat while they waited for dinner.

Jessa showed up just as the closing bells finished

tolling, trying very hard to look and act like he was already a noble. Unfortunately, he did it well. He wore clothes as fine as Montague's, rich greens and blues trimmed in gold, his hair braided and twisted into elegant knots that Rath would never be able to duplicate.

Montague motioned to the servant with the wine tray. "Good evening, Master Jessa. Good of you to join us. Now that all of you are here, I will inform Their Majesties and then call you to dinner shortly."

Once he'd gone, and the servants had faded off, silence fell among the little group. Jessa glanced at Rath and the others, then turned pointedly away from them to go examine one of the paintings.

"You'd think he'd at least try to be polite," Sarie muttered.

Benni snorted softly. "Has he bothered since we started? Don't expect it now. He's certain he'll win, even though so far I would swear his performance has been amongst the worst, except for maybe the first challenge where he finished right after you. How he's made it this far is a mystery."

"No, it's not," Sarie replied. "I'd bet my place in the tournament right now that he's cheating, and that he had something to do with that reprimand we all got. If he hasn't bribed or threatened his way through this whole thing, I'll eat my shoes. Wouldn't surprise me in the least that he paid to have someone killed."

Rath let the conversation wash over him, focused on the flavor of his wine, the memory of dancing and playing with Tress, tumbling into the sheets with him later.

"—house, Rath? Rath?"

He startled, staring blankly at Sarie. "I'm sorry, my mind drifted. What did you ask?"

She grinned at him. "Nervous a bit? Glad I'm not

the only one. I asked if your mother is enjoying her new house." She nudged him playfully. "She must be beyond excited. That was a smart boon."

"Money would have been smarter," Jessa said, turning away from the painting. "You could have bought a house and plenty more besides."

Benni shook his head. "I'd rather have security, and money is hardly secure, especially when you suddenly have a great deal of it. The house is a certainty, and no one can steal it."

Jessa's lips curled in a sneer. "Spoken like a true—" He broke off as a door opened and Montague swept in.

"Competitors, dinner is served."

Rath finished his wine and handed the cup off to a patiently-waiting servant, murmuring a thank you before he followed the others down the hall and into a dining room that made him want to turn and flee. His experience with eating was pubs, his own room, and feeding customers when they asked. None of those were adequate preparation for dining with the king and queen, no matter what manners the brothel had drilled into him.

He and the others knelt as they entered the dining room, heads bowed as formal introductions were made.

"Come sit, come sit," King Teric said congenially, and Rath was more than happy to let the others lead the way and sit as far away as he could get. Still too close, with only Jessa between him and the royal couple, but it was better than nothing.

Also at the table were Montague, Quinton, Sorrith, and a handful of other people whose names flew by him. He glanced surreptitiously at the king and queen. They were both beautiful, of course. Rath felt more inadequate than ever, hands twisting together in his lap.

His Majesty was tall and slender, hair cut so close

to his head that there was only the barest bit of tight curl to it, run through with a dusting of silvery white, and he had sky-bright blue eyes that did not look as somber or serious as Rath had expected. Something about him was familiar, but Rath could not say why.

Next to him, Queen Isara was even more beautiful, shorter than her husband and significantly larger. Her hair was bound up in heavy braids twisted together at the back of her head and run through with bright scarlet fabric that probably helped to keep it all up. Gold and red hearts were painted on her cheeks, red paint on her lips. Her skin was lighter than Teric's, whose skin was dark enough almost to be black. Her eyes were light brown, almost gold, and as warm and friendly as any Rath had ever seen.

Some of Rath's nerves eased, though that pricking at the back of his mind that something was familiar about King Teric would not stop nagging him.

"Master Rathatayen," Teric said, making him jump. "I hope you are doing well." He smiled gently.

Rath ducked his head, but then forced it back up. "I am, Your Majesty. Thank you."

"Good. How did you enjoy your visits to the villages assigned for your quest challenge?"

Rath brightened slightly. "I had a lot of fun. I'm fairly certain I'm too old to be drinking like that, but I hope Cartina does well at the market competition. I'd feel bad if I chose poorly."

Across from him, Sarie chuckled. "That sounds like the wine tasting I had to do in Harter. Were you as hungover as me for the three days following?"

"It certainly felt like it," Rath replied, not wanting to dampen the conversation by saying he'd been too worried about Teller and further attacks to care about his hangover. "Did we all have to do such judgings? I had pie, ale, and got to oversee a village frost fair and judge all sorts of things."

Benni gave a bittersweet smile. "I am sad I'm missing the frost fair in my home village. Favorite part of the year."

"Yes, there was a beautiful frost fair where I grew up," Isara said. "We were thinking of reinstating the frost fair here, to take place at the conclusion of the tournament."

Rath brightened. "Really? That would be fun— assuming people could get the time to go."

Jessa scoffed next to him. "People are already given plenty of holy days off."

"One more won't make much of a difference then, will it?" Sarie countered.

"That is what was decided, yes," Teric interjected, casting the barest hint of disapproval in Jessa's direction. "Most of those days are in the spring and summer months. There is little time away from work to be had in the winter. So it's all to the good, I say."

Jessa bowed his head, mouth slightly pinched. "Of course, Your Majesty."

Mouth widening into a happy grin, Teric said, "Speaking of fairs reminds me of one of my favorite stories about Isambard. He'd wanted to go to the summer fair his brothers were attending, but I forbade it. He declared he was going to go all by himself if he must, and I told him he wouldn't get very far without coin. So later, he snuck into my office when he thought it was empty, never noticing my secretary tucked back in the bookshelves that wrap around most of it, and stole two marks from a purse I'd left in my desk." He chuckled. "Of course, he felt so bad about stealing the marks, he didn't get any further in his scheming, and the next day he snuck back into my office to return them. Left them right in the middle of the desk, as though I or any of my servants would leave money out like that."

It could have been a coincidence. Any number of boys probably stole marks from their father's desks. It seemed like the harmless, defiant sort of thing that children would do. But the story was exactly the same in all the key points…

And *how* had it taken this long to realize why Teric looked so familiar? Tress had his nose and smile, that infectious grin that Rath surrendered to every single fucking time. That also explained Quinton's strange behavior, and about five hundred other things that Rath *really* should have noticed sooner.

Tress wasn't the son of a noble. He was Prince Isambard.

Rath's hand shook as he reached for his wine. He took a deep swallow, because there was no other way he was going to avoid screaming or cursing or jumping from his seat to go find the bastard and break his damned nose.

He barely remembered the rest of dinner, though he did his best to talk and smile and act like he wanted to be there. Whatever his murderous intentions toward their youngest son, the king and queen didn't deserve to be on the receiving end of Rath's temper, and neither did the other guests.

But it was a relief when he could finally leave.

"Master Rath!"

Rath groaned, but came to a stop as he reached his horse and turned back to face Quinton, mustering a smile that felt stiff on his face. "Yes, my lord?"

"You seemed troubled all throughout dinner. I wanted to make certain all was well and you were not being further troubled."

Some of Rath's anger slipped out. "Tell *Lord Tress* that he is fortunate our paths did not cross."

"Oh, dear," Quinton said quietly.

Rath bit back a hundred questions and accusations, turned, and swung up onto his horse. "My thanks to Their Royal Majesties, and everyone else, for a wonderful supper. Goodnight, my lord." He rode off before Quinton could reply, barely noticing that the guard who usually shadowed him did not follow.

Leaving his horse at the inn's stable, he went quickly to his room and changed out of his good clothes. He packed up all his scattered belongings and set them by the door, then sat on the bed to pull on his boots—

And stayed there, head braced in his hands as he went over every single moment he'd spent with Tress. With *Isambard.* Every stupid thing he'd said, the way Tress had gotten mad and defended the royal family.

He couldn't—he was going to *kill* that lying bastard. Why? Why had he lied? Why hadn't he just told Rath who he was? Why keep interacting with him at all when it was against the damned rules?

Rath swallowed, face flushing hot. He must have sounded so stupid, must have looked ridiculous, discussing the royal family, his disinterest, everything else that had tumbled out of his mouth because he'd thought he was talking to a noble. Tress had never said a word, just gone blithely along lying and evading like it was nothing.

The door creaked, loud as a clanging bell in the silence, and Rath looked up as Tress stepped into the room.

Rath let him step into the room and close the door, then surged from the bed and stormed across the space between them, grabbing Tress up and slamming him against the door. "You lying bastard! You fucking— you—tell me why I shouldn't break your fucking nose! I trusted you, I cared about you, and this whole *fucking time* you've lied to my face over and over—"

211

"It's not like that!" Tress said. "Please, Rath. I never meant to lie; it wasn't like that. Please."

Rath threw him to the floor and went to retrieve his bags. "Then what the fuck was it?" Oh, Fates. He'd just slammed and thrown around and yelled at a fucking prince. His knees nearly gave out, and he had to grab the bed briefly until the urge to laugh hysterically had subsided.

He was thirty-fucking-three years old. Far too old for all of this foolishness.

"Rath, please—" Tress stepped in close. "You look afraid of me, and that was exactly what I didn't want."

Rath gave an unsteady laugh. "I just threw you around like I would a dock worker doing something stupid and dangerous. You could literally—"

"Do a hundred things that you know damn good and well I wouldn't do!" Tress shouted. "Have I not made clear after all these weeks that I care for you?"

"Care so much you've lied to me this whole fucking time," Rath snarled, anger once more taking him over. "You lied to me about who you were, what you were. Let me wonder and worry why my lover was so excited that I might be marrying the prince and didn't seem to care at all that meant I couldn't be with *you.* I've been heartbroken for weeks, and you've just been lying and evading and probably have a fucking lark over it." He jerked away when Tress reached out for him. "Don't fucking touch me. I was worried sick about you when my father was murdered, and now I have to wonder: did someone who knew you see us together? Did they convey that you and I were already close? Is that why they jumped so quickly to murder instead of just beating me again?"

Tress's eyes filled with tears. "I didn't—"

"Didn't think of anyone but yourself and how fucking clever you are for getting away with your lies and evasions, with keeping your Fates-damned secrets."

"It wasn't like that," Tress said. "It got complicated. Please, Rath. Don't leave. Give me a chance—"

"I'm tired," Rath cut in. "I'm tired of my life being in upheaval, of never knowing what will happen next. My life might have been boring, but I worked hard for it and I had control of it. Since this stupid tournament, I've had no control over anything. I've just been rushed along and run over and struggling not to drown. I wanted *you*, but now it feels like I don't even know you, and why should I keep fighting in this stupid tournament for someone who couldn't even be honest with me?"

Tears fell down Tress's cheeks. "It wasn't like that. We had fun that first night and I thought that would be it, but I couldn't forget you. My every thought kept coming back to you. I thought I'd find you and have a bit more fun, but you just sunk deeper and deeper into me. I wanted you happy, but I couldn't tell you who I was because then they'd punish you for cheating if we got caught. It all got out of control and into a tangled mess, and I was hoping I could explain everything when it was over." He fell silent a moment, then in a barely audible voice added, "I really wanted you to win."

Rath grabbed up his bags and left, slamming the door shut behind him, flinching at the broken way Tress called his name but resisting the urge to return. He need to calm down and think, and he couldn't do either of those things while Tress was nearby.

Isambard. He needed to think of Tress as Isambard.

No wonder he'd never really known anything about Tress. Even without the tournament, it would have been the height of foolishness for Tress to let anyone know he was really a prince.

Rath lingered in the street, trying to decide where to go. His mother? Toph? No, he didn't feel like listening to other people right then, even people he loved and trusted.

Heaving a sigh, he headed for the temple, where a priest led him to a small bit of floor where he could sleep.

Rath pulled out some leftover bread and raisins snitched from the last meal he'd had with Tress. His stomach clenched as he remembered Tress throwing them at him, catching at least half in his mouth, teasing Tress for being such a spoiled brat that he'd waste food.

The way that had somehow turned into Tress feeding him.

He shoved a piece of bread into his mouth, but it stuck there, his mouth too dry to chew. He forced it down, then put the food back in his bag, leaned his head against the cold wall, and stared at the statues of the Fates in the middle of the sanctuary.

The one he faced was Sacred Temina, Goddess of Loving Fate, she who decided the relationships each person was destined for, be they romantic, platonic, parental, or otherwise. Unlike the other two goddesses, she was intersex, and of the three was said to be closest to those under her care. Many believed she walked amongst people from time to time.

He wished she would make it a bit more fucking clear what his fate was regarding Tress. Prince Isambard, whom Rath would marry if he made won the tournament. But he wouldn't even know if he'd made it to the last challenge until he arrived in the morning to hear the verdict.

What if he did win? Why would he want to marry Tress? Fates fuck him, *Isambard.*

"Tress," he said softly, the word echoing faintly in the mostly-empty room. No matter how many times he told himself it was Isambard, no matter how angry he was, he could only think of Tress as Tress. The spoiled brat who had tolerated Rath's rudeness the night they met. The man who had bought him for an entire night just so Rath could rest. Who gave him money and bought him clothes and took him to parties just because he wanted to spend time with Rath. Who'd never really asked for much of anything and had always been willing to give in to what *Rath* wanted.

Who'd eagerly and happily encouraged him every step of the way to try to win the tournament. Every single time he'd though Tress was pushing him away, Tress had been encouraging his own marriage.

Rath stared at the ring on his finger, heaved another sigh, then gathered up his belongings and left the temple to haul back to the inn.

But when he arrived, the room was dark and empty, save for a small, paper-wrapped package on the table, a folded piece of paper on top of it.

> *Rath,*
> *This was meant to be your wedding*
> *present. Whatever you choose to do, I*
> *would like it to be yours.*
> *Love,*
> *Tress*

Rath tucked the note away in his jacket, then ran his fingers over the delicate paper, decorated with flowers and ivy, far too pretty to waste on wrapping a present, surely. He picked it up, started to tug at the ribbon holding it all closed—then stopped. Set the package back down.

Bad luck to open a gift before the moment it was meant for, even if Tress had already decided that moment would never come to pass.

For which Rath couldn't blame him; Rath hadn't exactly been willing to listen or forgive. He was still angry. But maybe not as angry as he thought.

At the very least he could show up, see if he'd even made it to the final round. If he had...

He still didn't give a damn about marrying a prince. He did give a damn about losing Tress over stupid mistakes and misunderstandings and lost tempers.

Rath tucked the present into one of his bags, then stripped off his clothes and climbed into bed, but it was some time before his roiling thoughts and pounding heart calmed enough to finally let him sleep.

THE FINAL CHALLENGE

Rath wolfed down his breakfast as he headed for the stable, the guard who'd reappeared sometime in the night following close on his heels. The one day he'd needed to be awake on time, if not early, and he was bordering on being late.

He threw open the stable doors and strode inside—

Cried out when something slammed into his face and sent him stumbling back to crash on the courtyard cobblestones. Blood streamed from his nose, but Rath ignored it, save to use the sleeve of his jacket to staunch the worst of it. Behind him, the guard had thrown aside his own breakfast and drawn his sword, moving to stand in front of Rath as five men came out of the stable.

Rath scrambled to his feet, swearing when he saw three more men coming in the gate. "Fates curse you all."

The guard screamed as he lunged at them, one man not getting out of the way fast enough to avoid a blade to the gut.

Rath fled as the three from the street and one from the stable came at him, going until he was in a corner where they at least couldn't get behind him. He picked up a slop bucket that was half-full of sludgy run off and swung it out as hard as he could, catching one man dead in the face and sending him stumbling into another.

That didn't keep the other two from surging in to start swinging and kicking, but it was something.

Rath tried to protect his face, kicking out as best he could, blocking with the bucket where he was able, until it was yanked from his grasp. He used the chance to shove hard at the man pre-occupied with the bucket and bolted past him, careening into the other two so hard that all three of them went down in a tangle of limbs and pained cries.

Squirming, kicking, rolling his way free, and biting down hard on the hand that grabbed his arm, he got to his feet—and barely ducked a fist coming at him, throwing himself to the side to land on top of sacks of feed that had yet to be properly put away.

A bellow of rage gave them all pause, and then two more men were cut down by the guard. "Go," the guard snarled. "Get on your horse, hurry up. I'll finish tending these knaves."

Rath didn't waste time arguing, just bolted for the stable where his horse was thankfully waiting, held by a scared boy with a bruised cheek. Rath spared precious seconds to fumble out two pennies and pressed them into the boy's palm. "Get out of here. Find a city guard to bring help, then go see a healer, understand me?"

The boy sniffled, but nodded, and Rath swung up onto the saddle and rode out, forcing the men who'd come after him to get out of the way or get run over.

Rath tried not to let his emotions affect Thief, but he still trembled the whole way, vision blurring from tears, blood dried and sticky on his face. His nose felt like it had been smashed by a hammer. Probably a shovel. He was lucky the bastards hadn't thought to begin proceedings with a pitchfork.

He didn't slow until he reached the fairgrounds, and then only because there were too many people in his way. Cries and shouts went up as people who recognized him realized it *was* him, and then the crowds finally began to part.

Finally he reached the stage, where everyone else was already gathered and staring at him. He noted the spectator stands out of the corner of his eye, that something was different, but all his focus was on the stage. Dismounting, he headed for it, desperately trying to wipe and scrape away blood as he mounted the stairs. Brushing tears from his eyes, he blinked several times at Quinton. "Am I too late?" He winced as the words came out garbled and warped due to his damned nose.

But Quinton seemed to understand. She frowned. "You just barely made it. Who did this to you?"

"Men in the stables jumped us," Rath said, speaking each word slowly and carefully as more officials clustered around them. "The guard stayed behind to take care of them. I'm sorry for my unseemly arrival."

"You have no reason to be sorry," Quinton said. "Nobody was giving up on you until we had to. Go stand in line. I will take care of the rotten bastards who did this." She pushed him along, then strode off, bellowing out orders to guards who hastened to fall in line around her.

Rath shuffled over to stand with the other three. Sarie and Benni stared at him wide-eyed. Jessa didn't look at him at all, but his mouth was pinched with anger.

For the first time, Rath looked toward the spectators, smiling as he saw his mother. He blew her a kiss, waved to his friends clustered around her, then looked at the rest of the stands, which were more crowded than ever. It didn't seem like anyone had room to so much as shift a foot. And instead of being all the way at the top behind a silk screen, the royal family was arrayed right front and center.

Rath's throat felt scraped raw as he stared at Tress, sitting beside his mother and staring back at Rath with wide eyes, more emotions than Rath could follow flickering across his slightly-blurry face. He looked even more handsome than usual, dressed in court finery of green and gold, long heavy braids decorated with gold bands at the end, jeweled flowers scattered randomly about, gold hoops in his ears. There was a small gold something painted just beneath his left eye; Rath wished he knew what it was, wished he was close enough to touch it, kiss it.

"Your royal competitors!" Montague boomed out from behind him, making Rath jump.

Deafening applause filled the air.

Rath jumped again as a clerk touched his arm, but forced himself to relax when he saw the woman had bandages and other healing items. "Thank you," he said as she began to gently clean his face and apply a numbing ointment.

As the applause faded off, Montague continued. "Now to announce the two who will continue on to the final challenge. The first one is Rathatayen Jakobson!"

Rath startled, relief rushing over him, eyes stinging. He swallowed, tried to stand up straighter.

"Lift your arm," the clerk murmured. "Smile."

Rath did as she said, though the smile hurt—but everyone cheered even louder than before as he raised his arm, and they didn't quiet down until the horns finally trumpeted an order to do so.

Montague then bellowed out Jessa's name, of course, and Rath bowed his head to Sarie and Benni. They exchanged a strange smile, like they knew something no one else did, then nodded in reply to his bow. Benni then turned and let a clerk escort him from the stage. Sarie gave Rath a hug and gently kissed his cheek. "I'll be cheering for you," she said quietly. "Don't let that barn rat win."

"I won't," Rath said with a quiet laugh and waved farewell as she walked away.

"Your final competitors!" Montague bellowed out, and Rath grit his teeth against all the noise that was rapidly giving him a headache. His heart felt like it was going to shatter, it was pounding so hard. The only thing that kept him from going mad was the way Tress's gaze never left him.

Montague drew Rath and Jessa to the middle of the stage, then strode to the edge of it and bowed low. "Your Majesty."

Even the rest of the royal family, minus the queen, looked alarmed when King Teric leapt from the stands and strode to the stage. Though it couldn't have been much of a surprise, given that five guards moved with him without pause or hesitation.

Climbing the steps, Teric moved to stand between Rath and Jessa. He squeezed their shoulders, then strode forward to replace Montague at the front edge of the stage. "People of Dennarm, one last cheer for your remaining competitors!"

Once the latest round of cheering had died down, Teric continued. "The last and greatest challenge is my duty and honor to oversee. Throughout this tournament, we have tested the mettle, the honor, the kindness, patience, and dozens more qualities so vital to those charged with the care of the people." His voice rang out as clear as a bell, across a crowd gone silent and intent as they attended every word. "But the final decision for who joins my family belongs to those who will be trusting our champion with their care. Therefore, the final challenge of this tournament is The Heart of the People Challenge!"

"That's not—" Jessa said, then snapped his mouth shut.

Teric spun around to face Jessa and Rath. "Competitors, the challenge is simply this: all those with whom you've dealt with previously, the people of

221

this city, the representatives from the villages, the temple, and so forth, will cast their vote. Whosoever gains the most votes will be named champion. Do you understand?"

"Yes, Your Majesty," Rath said quietly, so nervous he could cry.

"Yes, Your Majesty," Jessa echoed, though he was much stiffer about it. For a merchant, he was terrible at hiding his thoughts.

Teric stepped back, motioning to Montague, who stepped forward and bellowed out, "Merchants, present yourselves!" When the seven merchants of the first challenge had arranged themselves in front of the stage, Montague said, "You were the first challenge, and so the first vote is yours. How do you vote, Seven Merchants?"

The merchant in the middle stepped forward, cleared his throat, and pitched his voice to be heard across the field. "We respect the talents of a man who did not have to waste hours of time to know how much money he would need to spend. We do not respect a man who would bully his own to get the best price. We give our vote to Master Rathatayen."

"You bast—" Jessa broke off as two guards grabbed him to keep him from launching himself off the stage and at the merchants, who bowed low to Teric and filed away.

Montague stepped forward again. "Your Most Holy Eminence, if you would grace us with your presence!"

The crowd in the stands parted, and Eminence Dathaten walked down the steps of the stands and across the field to stand in front of the stage, surrounded by a handful of priests. Montague bowed, then said, "You were the second challenge, Most Holy, and so I ask you and yours: how do you vote?"

Dathaten smiled. "We have faith in the kind heart

that risked life and livelihood to see to the well-being of others. We do not have faith in the man who goes through the motions, but has no depth. We give our vote to Master Rathatayen."

Rath let out a soft, disbelieving huff of shaky laughter.

Dathaten departed and Montague called for the village representatives. "You are the third challenge, honored leaders of our distant towns and villages. How do the distant reaches of the kingdom vote?"

"We welcome the one who visited his designated villages eager and sincere, happy to listen and learn and treat us as equals. We do not welcome the man who constantly reminded those he visited of his superiority and made it clear he wanted only to be home. We give our vote to Master Rathatayen."

Once they had gone, Teric said, "The next vote belongs to the castle."

He motioned to Montague, who stepped forward and cleared his throat, then once more bellowed out in his clear, far-reaching voice, "I speak for the castle—the guards, the servants, the clerks, and criers. The fourth challenge was for those of us who support the royal family, and we cast our vote with he who has always acted like a prince. It goes to Master Rathatayen."

The cheers that time took the horns several minutes to quiet down, and only with the assistance of Teric.

Rath couldn't *breathe*. He'd won it at three, if majority was what made the difference. He'd certainly won it at the fourth vote. Tears streamed down his face.

A hand settled heavily on his shoulder, squeezed it, and he looked up, but immediately shied away from the smile on Teric's face.

When the crowd finally quieted, Montague resumed speaking, voice somehow louder and clearer than ever. "The last vote goes to the people, all those gathered here today. If you have a vote, declare the name!"

Rath was absolutely certain that he never again wanted to hear so many people chanting his name that loudly ever again. But right then, it was the sweetest thing he'd ever heard.

When the crowd was finally wrangled into silence again, Teric grabbed Rath's wrist and lifted it. "Master Rathatayen, Royal Champion of the Tournament of Charlet! I think it's long past time his prize came down and rewarded him!"

Nobody even bothered to try calming the crowd at that point, and the noise and fervor only grew as Tress jumped over the edge of the stands and ran for the stage.

Teric chuckled and let Rath go, smiling a bit mischievously. "If you wanted to strangle your fiancé a little bit, I would not stop you. Just do not actually kill him."

Rath gave a shaky laugh, but before he could form a reply, his arms were abruptly full of Tress, who pulled back a moment later, only enough to cup Rath's face and kiss him.

The crowd at that point screamed and cheered so loudly that Rath was certain vocal cords must be permanently damaged, but he really didn't care about anything but Tress's kiss, the familiar arms that slid down to wrap around him.

"I'm sorry, I'm sorry," Tress muttered between kisses. He was panting when he finally tore away enough to properly speak. "I'm sorry, I didn't mean to lie. You came. I can't believe you came. I was so sure when you weren't here—" His words turned to garbled nonsense as Rath cut him off with another kiss.

Rath was going to regret all the kissing when he

could feel his banged up face again, but he just could not bring himself to care.

"All right, all right, save it for the wedding night," Teric said as he dragged them apart. "Isam, learn to share. There are other people who would like to congratulate him."

Tress laughed and stepped back as people began to climb the stage: Rath's mother, Toph, Warf, all his other friends, even Anta and her family, followed by the other competitors, most of whom congratulated him cheerfully, and the rest were at least polite.

He was so overwhelmed by people and steadily-returning pain, he barely noticed when they finally left the stage and were swept along to where tables and chairs had been arranged in various squares, jugglers already taking up their duties as people slowly milled about and found seats.

Rath watched it all go by in a blur as he was dragged into a small tent—an actual tent, not the open ones that were all he'd used so far. The flaps closed behind him, and Tress gently shoved him down into a chair. "You looked like you could use a chance to catch your breath."

"Yes, thank you." He looked down, feeling suddenly shy, or uncertain, maybe. "I'm sorry. I should have given you a chance to speak."

Tress made a soft noise and knelt in front of him. "You had a right to be angry. I almost told you a thousand times, but it always seemed like it was better if I didn't, for reasons that all seem stupid now. I didn't sleep all night because I was so scared you wouldn't come, and then you didn't show—" He swallowed, looked down, fingers curling restlessly on Rath's thighs. "Then suddenly, you were there, but you were hurt and that was my fault, too—"

"No," Rath cut in, covering Tress's hands with his

own. "I shouldn't have said that. The only people to blame for my father's death are the people who killed him. I was just tired and frayed and scared. I never thought I'd actually win. I'm still having trouble believing it."

Tress laughed, leaned up, and gently kissed his cheek. "I'm sorry. I bet your nose isn't very happy with me right now. Come on. Let's get you in less bloody clothes, see that nose is treated properly, and then it's time to celebrate. And tomorrow, neither one of us is leaving my bed."

"I like the sound of that," Rath said. He watched bemusedly as Tress went to work on his boots. "I don't even know what to call you. You've always been Tress to me. I can't wrap my head around Isambard."

Throwing the boots aside, Tress looked up. A star, Rath noted belatedly. It was a tiny, now-smudged star painted beneath his left eye. "Tressen is my middle name. No one ever uses it, so when I'm sneaking around the city like a spoiled brat, that's what I go by. My family calls me Isam." He smiled softly and leaned up to press another gentle kiss to Rath's cheek. "I like Tress, though. You're welcome to keep calling me that."

"Oh, I'd hate to take away your sneaking-around name," Rath replied.

Tress made a face as he rose. He held out his hands and tugged Rath to his feet, then went to work on removing his pants. "It's already ruined. Too many people will recognize me now, and Quinton has run out of patience, anyway. You should have heard the tongue-lashing she gave me when she heard you mention 'Lord Tress'. She's had to go in search of me more than once, and she wasn't anywhere close to amused when she found me." His face fell slightly. "She came to see me the night of the dinner, warned me you'd figured it out. *How* did you figure it out?"

"Your dad told the story of when you stole two marks from his office."

"That's what sunk me? Are you serious?" Tress scowled. "That's not fair."

"Fair? You're lucky your father didn't string you up by your toes, Highness," said a new voice, and they both turned to face Lord Quinton as she stepped into the tent and bowed.

"He probably has something much more evil in mind," Tress replied, rolling his eyes. "Did you come about the men who attacked him?"

"Yes, Highness, Master Rathatayen. We apprehended your assailants. They were hired by an intermediary, much like the men who killed your father, which means they were useless at finding a path back to the Tanner family. However, since the tournament is over, our good Friar was more willing to talk and gave us a couple of useful tips. Master Jessa and his father are currently under arrest, and acting rather sullen about it, but the bailiff thinks they will confess before the night is out. I came to see if you wanted a particular punishment levied. Given all the crimes they've committed, especially paying people to murder your father, the sentence will probably be execution."

Rath's eyes widened as Quinton and Tress looked at him. "Um. I don't want anyone else dead. What good does that really do in the end?"

Tress smiled at him, warm and fond, but it turned chilly as he turned back to Quinton. "Strip them of everything. Fine them so severely they will not have the time or ability to behave this way for a long time to come."

"I will convey your wishes, Highness," Quinton replied. She bowed again, then smiled at Rath.

"Congratulations, Master Rath."

"Thank you," Rath said.

Quinton turned and strode off, leaving them alone once more.

Tress sighed. "I'm glad that's over with. Do you want to bear witness when they're punished?"

"No, I have more important things to occupy my time," Rath replied. He stepped back when Tress got a look on his face that Rath knew very well. "None of that while there are literally thousands of people on the other side of that tent. Look how easily we were just interrupted by Lord Quinton. Stay over there so I can finally get dressed."

Tress pouted but conceded. "Fair point." He turned away and opened a small chest, pulled out the clothes that Rath remembered from the night of the dinner. "Will you wear them this time?"

"I suppose," Rath said with a smile. "Since I'm apparently engaged to a prince, even if it's the brattiest of the lot."

"I'm the brattiest, ha!" Tress replied. "You haven't met my brothers; you'll change your mind." He helped Rath into his clothes, then opened another box and pulled out jewelry. Rath tried to move out of reach, but Tress caught his wrist and, by way of a carefully placed kiss followed by a pretty pout, got his way. "I think I'll always prefer the pretty, rough and tumble drunk who teased me for reading in a pub, but you make a lovely prince."

Rath kissed him softly, wishing he could do more.

"Let's get that poor nose taken care of," Tress said and pulled out a small case containing healing supplies.

"You're remarkably self-sufficient for a hoity-toity. Does that come from years of sneaking around?"

Tress rolled his eyes. "We can actually dress ourselves, you know. But yes, stuff it." He quickly, but gently, tended Rath's nose, adding more ointment to help keep lingering pain at bay, smearing a cream around his eyes that he claimed would minimize the bruising. "You look a trifle beaten up, but still like my handsome champion." He brushed back a strand of hair. "I really do hate seeing you tired and beaten up and worn down all the time. I'm glad this is over with."

"We still have a celebration to survive," Rath replied, "but I am glad tomorrow will be quiet."

Smiling, Tress captured his fingers and kissed them, then tugged him back out of the tent and into the crush of the cheering crowd, pushing through it until they reached the high table. Tress sat down next to the queen, and Rath wound up between him and Sorrith, who beamed and clapped him on the shoulder. Around the rest of the table, he could see his mother and friends, who waved at him as he caught their eye.

When they were seated, Teric rose and lifted his cup. "To all the tournament champions!"

The cheers that time turned swiftly back to conversation and drunken revelry, leaving Rath mostly in peace to eat, drink, and be happy.

FIN

Coming Soon…

Quest of Fools

At the conclusion of the famous Tournament of Losers, humble dockworker Warf finds himself amongst the champions, set to marry Lord Marian, second son of the Earl of Bellowen. The marriage promises a life for his children that Warf never could have provided them on his own, a dream come true. Even better, his betrothed by Right of Tournament seems a genuinely good man sincerely interested in marrying Warf and helping to raise his children.

Not everyone feels like celebrating, however. Somebody wants Warf out of their way, and just days after Warf and Marian begin to build a new life together, Marian goes missing. Everyone says he's run off with his former lover, a woman he could not stop loving or leave behind. Everyone tells Warf to forget him, accept Marian is gone, take the money offered by the throne and build a new life with that. He'd be stupid to refuse it.

He'd be an absolute fool to go after Marian and do whatever it takes to bring him home.

About the Author

Megan is a long-time resident of queer romance and keeps herself busy reading and writing it. She is often accused of fluff and nonsense. When she's not involved in writing, she likes to cook, harass her wife and cats, or watch movies. She loves to hear from readers and can be found all over the internet.

meganderr.com
patreon.com/meganderr
meganderr.blogspot.com
facebook.com/meganaprilderr
meganaderr@gmail.com
@meganaderr

Made in United States
Orlando, FL
26 January 2024

42954240R00138